The End Note

THE ENDNOTE

A NOVEL ANDREW RIMAS

COMMON DEER PRESS

Published by Common Deer Press Incorporated.

Published in 2019 by Common Deer Press
3203-1 Scott St.
Toronto, ON
M5V 1A1

Library of Congress Cataloging-in-Publication Data
Rimas, Andrew.—First edition.
The End Note / Andrew Rimas
ISBN 978-1-988761-34-3 (print)
ISBN 978-1-988761-35-0 (e-book)

Cover Image: © Ellie Sipila
Book Design: Ellie Sipila

Printed in Canada

WWW.COMMONDEERPRESS.COM

Sigai, kuri neša mano širdį.

A rat crept softly through the vegetation
Dragging its slimy belly on the bank
While I was fishing in the dull canal
On a winter evening round behind the gashouse
Musing upon the king my brother's wreck
And on the king my father's death before him.

—T.S. Eliot, *The Wasteland*

Today the diameter of the observable universe is estimated to be 28 billion parsecs (about 93 billion light-years).

—Itzhak Bars, John Terning,
Extra Dimensions in Space and Time

For the perishable must clothe itself with the imperishable, and the mortal with immortality.

—1 Corinthians 15:53

Chapter One

The Royal Wheatleigh Jumeirah Banyan Resort &
Conference Center

THERE ARE EIGHT billion people on the planet today.
Tomorrow, there will be eight billion minus one. Or
there will be zero. The difference depends, in the next
few hours, on a solitary digit, a decimal of a decimal, a
mathematical jot.

One person over eight billion seems, by any reasonable arithmetic, lopsided. If you write it out as a
fraction, it takes about six seconds to sketch all the de-
nominator's little circles, trailing it out like a child's
drawing of a googly caterpillar.

$$1 / 8,000,000,000$$

And the single stroke for the numerator takes nothing at all.

I entered this equation on a winter morning three
weeks ago when I opened a box of cherrywood and

white satin and lifted out a black tablet embossed with the logo of the Anfort Foundation. It hummed to life and requested the honor of my presence at seven o'clock in the evening on December 28th, in the Palm Courtyard of the Royal Wheatleigh Jumeirah Banyan Resort & Conference Center.

Of course, I thought it was a mistake. But when I clicked the contact link, a voice assured me the invitation was genuine.

"Mr. Anfort approved each name personally," said the voice—female, Asian-inflected, proprietary software. "Is there anything more I can do for you today, Professor Adams?"

There was not. The invitation's digital concierge already knew enough about me to select a room with a view of the pool instead of one of the golf course, and to order the short rib entrée at the gala dinner. All I needed to do was confirm my preferred seat on the flight, aisle 9B, two checked bags included, and allow a minimum of six hours for airport security screening. The World Summit on Progress and Reconciliation thanked me for my kind response.

On the airplane, I opened my antique laptop to revise the notes for my committee sessions. They were based, mostly, on the research I had been grudgingly picking at over the course of the past twenty years—a general theory on Western literary thought. But as I looked at the words on the white screen, I felt an almost dyslexic blur, with the letters swimming out of their typeface into amorphous schools of tadpoles and twirls. I closed my device and shut my eyes.

Charles Anfort knew my name. And he knew it well enough to summon me to the most exalted summit since Olympus. It didn't make sense.

The airplane beeped a sing-song chime. Behind me, I heard the clink of the trolley from the steerage section. In the forward galley, a flight attendant, her mouth tight in concentration, dropped heavy red raspberries into flutes of fizzing prosecco. She looked all business, from her blonde, sensible hair-bun to her broad, sensible bottom. Below the sleeves of her jacket, I could see her forearms striped and wrinkled with bruises and brown burns. Scars, probably, from a life of scalding coffee, hot trays, and turbulence. A worker's scars. In the seat beside me, a trim black gentleman in a cashmere jacket dozed in silence.

I picked up the tablet one more time, running my finger over the Anfort Foundation's familiar logo: a lotus flower with thirteen petals. It was the mark of Charles Anfort, Sultan of Silicon Valley, the multi-billionaire with granny glasses and a wood rat's haircut. The man was a legend—or, rather, he was *the* legend. He had lived the hero's journey of our time. Act One: a banal boyhood in Boise, college fizzle, supreme self-regard against all evidence to the contrary, and the inkling of an idea that lay, like a golden key, just out of sight of everyone else on earth. Act Two: adulthood, the first tech venture and the years of Hobbes and Darwin, enemies defeated and allies betrayed, the temptation of settling for an easy buyout, an act of hubris, a very public fall. Act Three: redemption, earthly glory, riches beyond the dreams of Mammon, the purchase of starlets, spaceships, land masses, and the corpse of Steve Jobs. Act Four: respectability, the purchase of ideas and institutes, clinics and water treatment plants, handshakes with the pope, the eradication of malaria, rumors of a private moon base.

And now the curtain rises on Act Five. The planet is buzzing about something called the World Summit for Progress and Reconciliation—W.S.P.R. I first heard of it six months ago when the press breathlessly pronounced that "Whisper" would be "the greatest congregation of thought leaders in history." Catchphrases took root and, within days, the media bloomed with hope: "Whisper is going to reset the clock," "Whisper will update humanity's operating system," "Whisper is Ground Zero for the future." And, most memorably, "Whisper will heal the world."

So I found myself seated, for the first time in my life, in the front of the plane. Charles Anfort had plucked me from my forgotten basement at Rothbard College to sit on Whisper's "Committee on the Human Condition."

"This can't be real," said the dean when I handed her the invitation. "I don't mean to be dismissive, Magnus, but don't you think it's a prank? Maybe Jerry in Technical Services? He doesn't like you."

"No. I RSVP'd, and they confirmed my flight. It's hard to believe, but this is real."

She shook her head and gently passed back the tablet, as if it might scald my fingers. "I don't get it, then. No offense, really, but why on earth would they pick you of all people?"

"I haven't the faintest idea," I said. "I've been trying to figure that out since the damn thing arrived. Wait, Jerry doesn't like me?"

"Do you think they meant to send it to someone else?"

"Only if there's another Magnus Adams in the Digital Humanities Cluster at Rothbard College."

No doppelgängers, however, emerged from the particleboard woodwork of the faculty lounge. The real oddity was that the name Magnus Adams wasn't even well-known in the prescribed circles of academia. My published work had, since I launched my half-baked theory of literature years ago, dried into a trickle and was now more of a sucking wound.

I had squandered years of energy on the works of a minor school of 19th-century Romantics called the Naysayers. It wasn't a popular subject, even if their leader, a disreputable poet named Nicholas Crooke (d. 1848), had always enjoyed a modest vogue among addicts and suicides. Crooke didn't count as an important writer, or even a notably good one. He had an uneven grasp of meter. His images had the habit of melting into incoherence. But his drug binges had inspired many imitators and he had always touched a nerve with a specialty readership. A few of his poems consistently showed up in high school anthologies, namely, the juvenile, "Waking Did I Spy a Crow," and the unnerving "Succoth." But hardly anyone bothered reading his challenging material, best represented by the narrative cycle, *Songs of Ivory and Horn*. Sadly for my job prospects, this indifference carried over into the parched and thorny field of Crooke scholarship. It was barren ground on which a career might die.

Certainly, I never imagined Charles Anfort might count himself among the initiated. Perhaps he didn't. Perhaps, as the dean suspected, my invitation to the summit had all been a huge mistake.

Still, I dug my passport from out of a sock drawer and packed my two good suits into my one good suitcase. Two weeks later and 35,000 feet upwards, I reopened my laptop and scrolled through the latest news headlines:

HURRICANE ZIGGY CASUALTIES TOP ONE MILLION

GERMAN CHANCELLOR VISITS SOUTHERN FRONT: "NO ONE IS A CIVILIAN"

RAPTURE TERRORISTS CLAIM DALLAS/FT. WORTH "SUPER EBOLA" ATTACK

GLOBAL ELITE GATHER FOR HISTORIC WORLD SUMMIT FOR PROGRESS AND RECONCILIATION

"Would you care for a refreshment, sir?" said the flight attendant. The man in the window seat roused himself from his meditations.

"Just a club soda, thanks," he said in an undiluted Dublin lilt. He was perhaps ten years younger than me, and several magnitudes less rumpled. Even his shoes looked sleek and gleaming, like fresh-sloughed snakes.

"Of course. And you, sir?"

I accepted a jot of whiskey. As our attendant arranged

the drinks, the moment balanced between silence and the hesitation of first speech. Then the man cleared his throat and tipped the scales into conversation.

"It's got a pleasing look to it, that stuff," he said, nodding at my plastic tumbler. "Water of life, sunshine on barley and all that. But I can't abide the taste. I suppose color isn't everything." He laughed.

"Where in Ireland are you from?" I said.

"Lagos. But me mam was Dublin born and bred, and I boarded at Blackrock College with the Holy Ghost Fathers. The name's Jack. Jack Lekhanya."

"Magnus Adams." We shook hands.

"Great name, Magnus. Who gave it to you?"

"It's sort of vestigial. My mother's family is Minnesota Swedish."

"Well, that's highly exotic of them. I see you're a guest of Mr. Anfort's?" Jack nodded at the tablet peeking out of my carry-on, and I felt a flash of embarrassment. I had perhaps been too eager to flaunt it in public view.

"Yes. Sorry. I didn't really mean to..."

"Not at all. I got a golden ticket as well." He fished an identical tablet out of his satchel. "I'm with the U.N. in New York. Mostly, I mess around with computer models trying to predict stuff about rice and soybeans and potatoes. At the summit, they have me on the Agriculture and Fisheries Committee."

"I'm with the Committee on the Human Condition."

"Well that's a fine thing, to be sure. So how is the human condition these days?"

"I suppose the committee ought to figure that out."

He chuckled. "There's precious little hope of that, Magnus, unless you already have the answers up your sleeves."

"Fair point," I conceded, but I didn't want to get drawn into discussing the inconsequence of my work. "I guess most people in my business would say that the human condition is the same as it's always been. Maybe a little faster and louder is all."

"We have better stuff."

"Oh, yes. But our condition is still the usual mess. First we're born mewling and puking, then we whine like schoolboys."

"'And then the lover sighing like a furnace, with a woeful ballad made to his mistress's eyebrow.' Sure, I remember my Shakespeare. Seven stages of man. Fifth form, Mr. Peters's class. Grand stuff, that. I can still recite Macbeth's dagger speech word for word."

"Very impressive. But you must know all about the state of humanity," I said, volleying the subject back into his court. "They say we are what we eat, no?"

Jack chuckled and launched into a yarn about falling global production of millet and water tables in northern China. "It's a challenge," he said. "But every problem has a solution. It's just a matter of getting people to think rationally."

I couldn't help but laugh, but then I noticed his rueful smile. "Oh, you were serious," I said.

"I'm afraid so. Generally speaking, I'd say it's in the social interest not to starve everyone to death. What

8

Adler called *gemeinshaftsgefuel*. It's not like the world's inhabited entirely by lunatic monsters."

"You and I have clearly been watching different news stories," I said.

As the airplane slipped toward pale veins of sunrise, I remembered the first time I encountered a line of Nicholas Crooke's, scrolling through an outdated literature compendium as a boy, my blood inked with longing. The line read, *"Fell dreams rake o'er the yielding clay of thought."* This seemed a reasonable encapsulation of disquiet, and it echoed with me then on the plane as Jack snored lightly, a silk eye-mask shielding his slumber from the wink of the lavatory sign.

Fell dreams. I trawled through a stream of troubles and regrets, my thoughts catching on stubs of recollection. Faces, names, dates. Over the years, I had cordoned off whole sweeps of my cortex, purposefully committing these memories to darkness. But on that flight I drifted loose, touching on events that, like torn canvases, my past left spoiled and ripped. Then, floating up to the surface, I succumbed to a swarm of mundane niggles: unwritten papers, undialed calls, unkept doctor's appointments, the unpaid bill for my cognac-of-the-month club.

We landed some eight hours later. The glassy, gargantuan airport terminus reminded me of another line of Crooke's: *"Black shadows spring from brightest light."* From the porthole, I glimpsed rows of sand-dappled tanks lurking on the tarmac.

"Ladies and gentlemen, you may turn on your

devices," said the flight attendant. "The local time is 6:22 am, and the outside temperature is currently thirty-four degrees Celsius with highs expected in the low forties. We hope you've enjoyed your journey with us today. On behalf of your entire flight crew, it has been our pleasure to serve you." Her cantillation ended in a crackle.

As we stewed in our seats, Jack telephoned friends, coworkers, and business contacts, volubly pleased to speak with them. I reread a batch of old emails. After an hour or two, the door clunked ajar, and we wrestled with the luggage bins. Stomping up the gangplank, we trudged quietly past ranks of masked soldiers lining the concourse. I could see the passengers' reflections in the soldiers' visors—us, bleary and greasy in nightsweat; them, silent in black Kevlar. Their dogs wore matching armor, straining their nostrils but otherwise sitting still, inhaling the instinct to lunge.

Security only thickened past Customs and Immigration, with the terminal in a state of frantic, noisy alert. Loudspeakers barked, SWAT teams beetled across the mezzanine, and armored troop carriers shuddered and gusted in the handicapped parking spaces. Above, the hot daylight chugged with helicopters.

"They're not messing around," said Jack, appearing beside me. "Do you think this is all on account of us?"

"I guess so. There are some pretty big names showing up at the summit. They must think Rapture is going to pull something."

"Of course they are. Those bastards would be mad

to miss the chance. What's the guest list now? Sixty heads of state, all the richest people on Earth, Mickey Mouse, and the Blessed Virgin herself?" Then a swirl of liveried attendants stripped my suitcase away, and I found myself shunted into a gleaming black Otto car.

I had never been in such a luxurious model, a cocoon of creamy leather and polished black screen, the seats thrumming with haptic sensors, rollers, and massaging nubs. The instant the door clicked shut, the Otto welcomed me by name and peeled away from the curb. In seconds, it was speeding through a blur of colorless haze and concrete. Before the windows darkened to shield my eyes, I saw that, outside, the world looked overlit and overcooked.

We skimmed through concrete and dust-clouds for about an hour while I scanned a touchscreen for any news containing the words "Rapture," "World Summit," and "death toll." Nothing came up. Then I felt the car slow to about 90 miles per hour. From the tinted backseat window, I could see a gate like a monolith of black graphene in a 40-foot wall crowned with curls of razor wire. A camouflaged tank sat, idling lazily, by a candy-striped security post. We slowed down as the gate swung open, exposing a brilliance of green.

"We will be arriving in a moment," said the Otto. "I hope you've had a pleasant journey, Mr. Adams." Then it snaked along a red-brick road framed by fronds and creepers. I glimpsed bursts of emerald quetzals and expressionist macaws, as well as an outrageous flamingo in a patch of roadside ooze. We swung under a cyclopean limestone portico, a rough primeval ruin like the entrance of Mycenae or Jotunheim, but with security cameras and floodlights roosting in its nooks. The car door clicked open.

"Thanks," I said, stepping into a wash of searing whiteness that felt like being doused in hot bleach. The air shimmered with heat and petroleum exhaust. My stubby suitcase in tow, I plunged through a set of revolving doors, into the chill of the resort's Great Pavilion.

At once, cool air peeled the shirt away from my swampy back, and I smelled cherry blossoms on a tickling breeze. The lobby was enormous and put me in mind of one of Crooke's happier laudanum binges. A giant silicon dome blazed with starlight, brighter than a cloudless sky over a mirror-calm sea. Red-tailed comets and plumed serpents drifted through the stars like trails of bright vapor. Underneath, hologram butterflies and fire-winged swallows flitted and fell in golden shimmers among the hundreds of guests pooling around the reception stations. At eye-level, VR screens mimicked an enveloping landscape of spruce trees sighing on breezy grass slopes, while angel voices murmured, in every major commercial language, about a special credit card offer for premier level guests. A wispy young woman in a white sheath dress appeared in my path.

"Professor Adams?"

"Yes, that's me."

"Welcome to the Royal Wheatleigh Jumeirah Banyan

Resort & Conference Center. I trust you had a pleasant connection from the airport. My name is Alia. Would you care to leave your luggage with me while I expedite your registration?"

Alia left me deep in a rum cocktail and a leather armchair while she scanned my documentation. Across the lobby, I saw Jack laughing and slapping backs with a throng of beaming colleagues. They flashed expensive dentistry and looked awash with vitamins. They were friends, no doubt, from the rarified stratosphere of international governmental organizations.

It was funny how bureaucrats had climbed up the social food chain. As a boy, I always thought of them as egg-shaped men, slick with failure, or thorny spinsters bent over their wasted ovaries. They simply weren't glamorous. Back then, kids played at rogue superheroes or rebel captains, cowboys who rode the bucking system until it broke. Today, they pretend to be systems administrators and risk analysts. This makes sense. Centuries ago, everything people thought and did was steeped in the governing truth that the world was absurdly messed up, and an afterlife in the lap of Christ was all that really mattered. To deal with sin and Saracens, you needed knights in armor. Today's governing truth is more complicated: The world is still absurdly messed up, but overpopulation, climate change, and economic inequality are all that really matter. To deal with macroeconomics and large-scale vulnerability assessments, you need technocrats with spreadsheets.

The difference is data. The world isn't made of soil and rock and water anymore. It's made of information. And the world always gets the heroes it deserves.

My phone vibrated with a new text. The sender's ID was, vexingly, "Unknown." The message was more vexing still. It simply read: *You don't belong here.*

I looked around. There were hundreds of people walking around, laughing, communing with their devices. Alia tapped dutifully on her screen. My phone thrummed again.

It was the same anonymous sender. *You should never have received an invitation.* Then: *You're an intellectual fraud.*

"Professor Adams?" It was Alia. Nearby, a coterie of hereditary monarchs grinned under a battery of flashing cameras. "Your room is ready, sir. I just need your signature, please."

I absently signed her pad and followed her past the King of Thailand and the Emir of Qatar, down a wide, warmly-lit hall, spongy with gold carpeting. Rows of elevators dinged merrily.

"Your itinerary has been uploaded to your invitation tablet," she said. "If you have any questions at all, I would be most happy to help. Do you have dinner plans this evening?"

Her tone suggested an invitation, or so I thought. "Um. No."

"If you're in the mood for lighter fare, may I recommend the Asana Lounge? Or Chakra, one of fine dining establishments, is excellent if you feel like something more traditional. I'd be delighted to make a reservation."

"That's alright."

She spooled through a monologue about wellness centers, pool hours, and the award-winning holistic spa. The entire time she spoke, I noticed that she was able to keep her eyes smiling while fixed unwaveringly ahead. I also noticed that her dress revealed the full splendor of her golden back, and her dark hair swished against the root of her spine.

My phone buzzed again. *Stop staring at her ass you filthy old goat. She's half your age.* And that was the moment it fully dawned on me that, even in this busy wasteland, I was not alone. I looked around again and saw soft crystal lights, polished stone, and dozens of what looked to be prosperous network scientists, none of whom I knew.

"Would you like to follow me to your room, Professor?" Alia smiled, stretching her lips a little farther than seemed natural. Her teeth had the same sheen as the marble in the elevator vestibule. I glanced back at the crowd to see laundered sheikhs, turbaned Sikhs, and ladies in ruby saris. Cameramen shoved their lenses at junta generals dressed like boxy Christmas presents in ribbons and gold brocade. An actress famed for her brood of adopted children posed next to her husband, an industrialist famed for his abuse of child labor. I recognized the bloated trapezia of an Olympic swimmer, the bleached hair of a Korean pop star, the spectacles of a movie director who had been accused of rape in three countries. I recognized a great many people, but I didn't know anyone there. Unless someone stood hidden behind one of the pillars or jungle fronds, I couldn't imagine who might be sending me these texts.

"Professor?" said Alia in a firmer coo. I let the elevator door ding shut on the human miscellany. The panel showed the numbers 1 to 99. Alia pressed 30.

You are a total disgrace, buzzed my phone, and then we swooped into light, up thirty flights above a diamond necklace of swimming pools, above a crushed velvet golf course, above sandbags and watchtowers, even above the falcons circling in the furnace currents of the desert beyond.

I'd lied to Jack Lekhanya on the airplane. I do know something about the human condition: Impermanence is our permanent complaint. If you went back 17,000 years to chat with one of the cave painters of Lascaux, he would explain he was elegizing a bygone day in the Upper Paleolithic, back when the aurochs were taller, the antelope more fulsome, and the megaloceroses had bigger antlers. And now, for the first time, human regret is scientifically justified. From atmospheric CO_2 levels to meteorological drought measurements to sea surface temperatures, we now possess the data to prove that the world is completely screwed.

When I was a boy, my parents made an annual pilgrimage to Uncle Ole and Aunt Ingrid's country property, a converted seminary on the shore of Minnesota's

Teakettle Lake. It was a skewed, redbrick Victorian with a crown of leaning chimneys, its creaking insides riddled with nooks and curious staircases, its attic windows exhaling nightly streams of bats. My mother's family, granite-faced sets of Andersons, Jensens, Carlsons, and Bergs, used it as their summer headquarters, camping out in the many bedrooms, sometimes two to an ancient, springy bed. The screen doors were always banging shut to the whoops of children, and the kitchen always simmered with the grandmotherly scents of boiled potatoes and fried fish. A trail sloped past the sleepy beehives to a rickety boathouse amid the sloppy lily pads, while a gravel path led a quarter mile along the shore to a crescent of sand where the women drank vodka and tomato juice while the menfolk kicked and dove in the bottle-green pond. There were tree houses and frogs to snatch from the mud and two nervous horses in a paddock. In my memory, it was a bright dream of eternal July, even on days washed out by pale Midwestern rainstorms.

It was during such damp afternoons that I explored the house's jumbled bookcases and boxes of yellowed magazines. As the rain drummed on the windowpane, I would lie in my cot, immersed in tales of Arthur and his knights, Leonidas and his brave Spartans, Chamberlain's stand at Gettysburg, and the first wave at Omaha Beach. Those old stories kindled in me a boy's romance for gallant dying, the pang for beautiful sacrifice on a windswept field with banners lifted high unto the final cannonade. Uncle Ole noticed me mooning around, so he helped me navigate the shelves. It was Ole who led me to Beowulf's plunge in the mere, to Roland's horn at Roncevalles, even to *The Story of Burnt Njáll* with the outlaw Gunnar's last stand at his homestead door.

I remember Ole in those days, his stubby legs thrust under the kitchen table as he told dirty jokes, or puttering, in goat-leather gloves, among his bees. He was a deep font of family lore, which he would dispense when we went hunting mushrooms, baskets in hand, under the cool pines. From him I learned about Andersons past. There were farmers and cranks, and heroes like the ones in my storybooks: George and Conrad, who fought in the first war, and Francis, who died in the second. There were villains, too, like the pretty young wife of a great-grandfather who ran off with the local minister and perished in the rubble and burn of old San Francisco, struck down by the justice of God.

It was Ole, too, who taught me how to pin a worm on a hook, threading its wagging finger through the cruel rust. He taught me, too, the likely haunts of trout. I was no older than six when, standing on the end of the pier, he helped me pull up a magnificent catfish, fierce and regally whiskered. I wrestled it into a bucket, where it shuddered and flapped, a royal beast among the little bass we'd been snagging all afternoon. Ole carried the slopping bucket up to a wooden table by the boathouse. On the stained tabletop lay a knife and a pointed brown rock.

"This is real important, Mags," said Ole. "You have

to be quick. Fish are just stupid things, but they feel scared, same as you or me. They suffer in the air, same as you would if a big catfish held you underwater. So always end it quick, before they know what's happening."

He grabbed a curling, rainbow-scaled creature from the bucket and, with two deft swipes, took off its head and flicked the innards on the green water.

"There. No pain, and now it's ready for the pot. The big one's yours, Mags. Want me to do it for you?" I shook my head. Sir Lancelot wouldn't be scared of gutting a fish. Ole nodded, and, wiping his big hands on a checkered rag, he stepped aside from the butcher's block. From the bottom of its white plastic prison, my catfish calmly wagged its tail and stared.

"Hold it firm," advised Ole. "And finish it off like I showed you." With both hands clenched hard, I managed to get hold of the oily scales, and, a minor Hercules wrestling his Nereus, pinned my flopping catfish onto the tabletop. Gills flaring, it twisted and thrashed, rocking the jittery surface. I could feel it sliding through my left-hand fingers as my right fumbled for the knife.

"Steady now, Mags. You can do it," said Ole, but my hand sent the blade spinning off the table. Panicked, I grabbed the pointed stone and slammed it down on the glossy flat skull, just above the silver coin of its eye. It caved in a burble of goo. But the fish kept thrashing. I struck again, splitting the disc, then twice more until the animal stiffened, its head a pink mash.

Ole appraised the mess. "That's alright, Mags. You did it quick. I'm sure it didn't feel anything. Next time, you'll do it clean. Come on, then, your aunt will want these for the stewpot."

For a dozen summers thereafter, my family returned to Ole and Ingrid's country house, but every year it underwent some sort of change. First, the sky curdled and the bees died. Then the woodlands turned brown and dry, or white and skeletal as marsh water spoiled the soil. After a few years, the blooming clouds of mosquitoes made even the daylight hours a maddening, scratching hell. Season by season, Teakettle Lake thickened with burping algae while its waters curdled in the breathless heat. Eventually, the house passed its summers shuttered and empty.

The last time I saw it was on Thanksgiving, a year or two into my college days. I was no longer a boy dreaming of knight errantry but an arrogant young scholar earning a fancy degree, certain in my deep readings of theory and criticism. Ole, too, had changed. Age had leached away his goodness. Gone was the wink and double entendre, the playful pat on his wife's backside. His mind had calcified around the TV tropes of hoodlum blacks, killer Muslims, and the end of times. He steeped himself in odious blogs, vented to online strangers about the cyclicality of the Earth's climate, and hardened in his conviction that liberals had betrayed all that was sweet and proper about our patria.

As the turkey carcass diminished, Ole grew hotter with each splash from the vodka bottle. After he let out some indefensible bray about gas chambers, I called him out. I told my old uncle that he was a racist and a fool.

"What happened to you?" he yelled back. "You have no respect! In my house, you have to show me respect!"

"I respect people who deserve it," I snapped back. Ole lurched up and, eyes afire and nose adrip, flung his arm in a wild, backhanded smack. He misjudged the distance and swung wide, the momentum toppling him sideways across the dinner table. Then an eruption of shrieks, spills, and clattering china, and the inexorable slide of the turkey as the tablecloth dragged floorward. I will always remember Ole's dumb rictus, ringed with spit, and the feeling of stones filling my chest as I watched him thrash in the litter of bones, shouting for someone to pick him up.

They say that after the incident with the apple, God set the angel Uriel to guard the gates of Eden with a giant flaming sword. God really overdid it. A wristwatch would have worked just as well, for time only points in one direction. Time tells us we can never go back.

Alia led me down a grand, cream-colored hallway awash with sunlight and jotted with smooth, abstract sculptures of geometry and genitals. Her heels clicked in the silence.

"May we expect the pleasure of your company at this evening's welcome reception, Professor Adams?"

"Yes, of course. I wouldn't want to miss the chance to meet Charles Anfort."

She smiled and pushed open a mahogany door. The suite was several times the size of my apartment at home. Picture windows shone with white sky and a gray, feathery horizon, and a glass door opened onto a shaded balcony overlooking the aquamarine gleam of a swimming pool. A chandelier fell in crystal droplets over a marble-topped dinner table, while sofas like prize bulls herded around a giant black screen. The bedroom was a silk seraglio, with gold canopy and tasseled pillow.

"The resort is equipped with the latest in SmartLife technology," said Alia. "Once you're logged in, you can use your phone to control everything from the curtains to the humidity to the bath faucets. You're scheduled to attend tomorrow morning's plenary session. I can make you a reservation for breakfast or have it delivered to your room. Mr. Keyes's opening address begins at eight-thirty."

"Sorry, what was that?"

"May I make you a reservation for eight o'clock?"

"No, the other part. About the opening address."

"Mr. Keyes is scheduled to deliver it at eight-thirty."

"David Keyes?"

She glanced at her tablet. "Yes. David Keyes from Mackinaw Labs. The title is 'Why We Fight: The Human Imperative in an Age of Crisis.'" She smiled again. Then, "Professor, is everything alright?"

"Yes, fine. Thanks. You know, don't worry about breakfast. Thank you. I think I'm going to lie down for a bit."

She discretely took her leave, pausing only to adjust a vase of white lotuses on the dining table. I sank flat onto the bed, the plush comforter exhaling slowly around my ears.

There were eight billion people in the world. Eight billion people clamoring to be heard. And yet David Keyes was the one giving the summit's opening speech.

One of the less reliable biographies of Nicholas Crooke recounts an anecdote, perhaps apocryphal, in which the poet and his longstanding rival, the balladeer Arthur Napier, competed for a commission from Charles Manners-Sutton, the Archbishop of Canterbury. The archbishop had offered to pay £25 for an original verse to commemorate the completion of work on his cathedral's southwest Arundel Tower, and Crooke and Napier were both young, ambitious, and cheap. Per his habit at the time, reflecting his short-lived "Ottoman Period," Crooke arrived for his interview wearing a set of ostentatious pantaloons and a dervish headscarf. He was kept waiting for a long time before Napier emerged from the drawing room, looking pleased.

"You may go home, Nicholas," said his enemy. "The archbishop no longer wishes to consider your bid for the commission. I have just been awarded the work, and at double the promised fee."

Crooke, who was famously intemperate, could not let this insult pass unaddressed. Storming into the archbishop's office, he unleashed a torrent of scorching profanities. As the old priest listened patiently, the poet worked himself into mounting flights of rage, threatening death, demoniac tortures, and the most imaginative acts of physical defilement. Reaching a crescendo, he leveled a quavering finger and vowed the vigorous, and repeated, debauch of the clergyman's elderly wife.

The archbishop shook his head in amazement. "It's uncanny," he said. "Just five minutes ago, a gentleman bet me £50 that the next person I saw would be a raving lunatic in pajamas."

The point being, the universe may be indifferent and cold, but it's always other people who actively screw with you.

My phone chirruped again.

You are a pissant nothing. A fizzing blob of cancer cells. A gangrened dick useless even as a medical specimen. Go fuck yourself.

I texted back: **David I'm blocking you.**

How on earth did David Keyes know I was at Whisper? We hadn't spoken in nearly ten years. More to the point, why would he have sought me out for the sole purpose of sending me abuse? David may have been my enemy, but he wasn't unhinged.

Five seconds later, my phone buzzed. It was, again, from an untraceable number.

I'm not David, it read. But I know what you did to him.

Chapter Two

Causality and Correlation

OF THE FOLLOWING events, which do you think are directly related?

The publication, nearly two hundred years ago, of Nicholas Crooke's "Lines Composed in the Dead Light Hours at the Dane John Mound in Canterbury, Having Overpaid a Pair of Rapacious Strumpets," commonly abbreviated to the less unwieldy "Dead Light."

The establishment, twelve years ago, of Rothbard College's Institute on Cultural Creativity.

The production, ten years ago, of the pilot episode for *Squidface and McGunn*, a buddy-cop show about the adventures of a maverick Los Angeles detective and his sidekick, a Lovecraftian horror from beyond the veil of human comprehension or sanity.

The collapse, at approximately the same time, of David Keyes's marriage.

The year is 1831, the scene is Canterbury Cathedral, ancient and storied, its stones hallowed by a thousand years of pilgrims seeking unction and answers. Nicholas Crooke slinks along the apse, mesmerized by the jeweled dapple under a window of St. Michael. A drone from the quire indicates that services are in progress. He moves closer, cupping an ear to catch the Kentish cadence of the pastor reading aloud the Parable of the Sower.

The pastor talks of seeds devoured by birds, seeds withering on sun-cooked stone, seeds curled with choking thorn. He raises a knowing eyebrow to the flock, commending his hunched listeners: "And other fell on good ground, and did yield fruit that sprang up and increased; and brought forth, some thirty, and some sixty, and some an hundred. And he said unto them, He that hath ears to hear, let him hear."

Seeds, in the poet's mind, take root. That night, lying under a half-moon gleam in the gardens by the old city wall, Crooke stares up at the wheeling stars. He can still taste the floral bitterness of his evening opium ball. A pair of whores—one too young, the other too old to cost the full market price—lie beside him. His pride has recovered from his shaming at the archbishop's house, his sense of his own powers is restored to its full lunar swell. Now his mind courses with revelation. He sees clear the lineaments of eternity. The whores, for their part, are numb to their fingertips with gin.

"Do you see it?" says the poet. "In the deep between the stars?"

The older woman is kind and strokes his cheek. "What do you see, my beautiful boy? Is something troubling you? You see something bad in the dark?"

"Ah, leave him alone, Jess," jeers the younger whore. "He needs to sleep it off is all."

"Sleep no more!" cries Crooke. "Sleep that knits up the raveled sleave of care, the death of each day's life, sore labor's bath." The prostitutes roll their eyes, but Crooke fails to notice. He remains rapt on the sky. "I will not sleep this night, or any other, until I put the darkness into words." Elbowing away the ladies, he staggers to his knees. "I must go at once! Greatness calls. Adieu, foul succubi! You shall no more sap my genius nor leech my vigorous juices!"

"Leech your what?" exclaims the younger whore. "We didn't leech nothing. You said you'd buy us each a bottle of Nicholson's."

Now Crooke is on his feet, reeling like a sailor on a bucking deck. Leaves cling to his hair, and his eyes burn with purpose. "O cankered trollops, this night I have seen Creation's truth! The scales have fallen, and blackness eternal opens wide before my sight. Go from here knowing that you have witnessed my epiphany!"

"What epiphany?" says the older whore, turning suspicious.

"I have seen God, and He is the space between the stars. The universe is an endless pit, lifeless and insensate, and Man is not even the merest mote of dust to swirl in't."

The whores shift uncomfortably. The younger one seems to find something caught in her eye. Eventually, the older one speaks. "You owe us a half crown."

"What?"

"It's what we agreed."

"Those are London prices," sniffs Crooke as he pays them. "It's outright robbery, especially considering I bought that meat pie you so avidly absorbed." They stick out their tongues. "Fine. I consign you both to the devil. Now I must depart. I am summoned to my destiny!" And he lurches away in the darkness.

Between midnight and sunrise, Crooke feverishly scribbles out the 36 lines of decasyllable quatrains that would, with substantial editing, comprise his earliest masterpiece, "Dead Light." Although it is little read today, later, more popular Naysayer writers liberally purloined its imagery—Rampling's dream of outer space in "Elegy for a Termite" is more or less a direct theft, as are Donetti's boneyard landscapes in *The Hollow-way*. I believe that the poem is Crooke's cleanest break with the derivative Romanticism of his juvenilia, and is the first full flower of his powers.

My favorite stanzas are the final two:

I watch cold hatchings in the endless deep,
Taste ash that falls from distant ember stars.
Oneiroi drool and gibber in my sleep,
Gone mad in space 'twixt Jupiter and Mars.

In blackened rags, dead angels gidd'ying fall
Through ceaseless void, past suns for eons blind.
In timeless waste we all forever crawl,
Un'compassed by our Lord's demented mind.

I recall the frisson of recognition I felt when, as a pimpled youth, I first read them. Here, I saw, was a writer who, even two centuries past, had grappled with the only genuine truth facing a thinking, modern human being. Here was a writer who knew, even before the current iteration of the telescope, that in the entire 98 billion light-year diameter of the universe, statistically zero percent is friendly to life. It's not even rudimentarily polite to it. I do not exaggerate when I say that the whole of the universe—every gamma ray, every isotropic particle—is insanely murderous. Physics itself is a cosmic axe-wielding maniac. The universe's entire existence confirms the singular fact that death is the natural state.

And it's not only space that wants to kill us. Time is the bloodiest butcher of all. Given time, everything dies. Three score years and ten, a mayfly's day in the sun, a redwood's thousand years. Every cell bobbing in the ancient ocean soup, every paramecium, every brontosaurus, every ten-mile mushroom buried in the loam: all must perish as surely as the protagonist in a Shakespeare tragedy, but with considerably less explication.

We all know this, deeper than at gut-level, etched in the links of our DNA. Death is our species' passion. Sex can't hold a candle to it. How many Pyramids of Giza or St. Peter's Domes have we raised in worship of procreation? Sure, we have the Virgin Mary and baby Jesus, our culture wars, our obsession with the mechanics of what part of the anatomy goes where and with whom.

But these are relative afterthoughts. Death's opposite gets few Corinthian architectures of logic, few constructs of philosophy, and no theistic religions at all.

Tens of thousands of years ago, our nameless ancestors made fertility dolls. These bulbous, faceless carvings of breast, butt, and belly, are smooth save for the meaningful cleave of the labia. They look so alien to us, these swollen Venuses. Why did the ancients make them? Was it to help the crops grow? Pray for babies? Salute the vagina? We can scarcely imagine what they were thinking.

No. Between the two siblings of life and death, death is clearly the favorite.

I silenced my phone, but at precise 45-second intervals, my nameless enemy texted me the single word, *Balls*. This had been going on for an hour and a half. From my vantage at the shaving mirror in my splendid marble bathroom, I could see the little windows pop, perfectly timed, on the device that I had set on the edge of the bathtub. I had blocked the number, but every time I did, the texts returned from another unknown set of digits. It occurred to me, and not for the first time, that I may be going insane.

Embedded in the shaving mirror, a little screen played news footage of the latest bioterror attack—Moscow this time. The killers had used U731, an airborne strain of super-ebola that's undetectable for the first twenty-four hours. During the next twenty-four, it speeds though a lightning progression of fever, vomiting, internal and external hemorrhaging, organ failure, and death. I kept a distracted eye on the carnage as my razor mowed swaths of smooth pink out of the rippled, white surface of my cheeks.

The shaving cream felt cool and pleasing, but the sight of my face underneath evoked a familiar disappointment. I looked like a corrupted steak. My jowls sagged fleshy and loose, pillowing over the contour of my jawbone. The crinkles around my eyes tightened into little accordions of skin, and their underhanging pouches had swollen purple and ripe. There were pinpricks of mysterious discolor, eruptions and craters left by time's creeping barrage. In the crevices of my nose and the untamed hedges of my eyebrows, silver ropy hair lashed out at the world, while the stuff on my head turned the color of cigarette ash.

Balls.

I buttoned a fresh blue shirt and clenched a belt around my midriff, which still felt swampy from the plane. *Balls.* I knotted a yellow tie speckled with little woven whales. *Balls.* I swiped a cloth across the toes of my loafers. *Balls.* Then I was ready to go downstairs to the reception, where Charles Anfort would welcome all of his honored guests. And one of the most honored was David Keyes.

Balls.

The time is twelve years ago, and the scene is a noisy brasserie as conversation volleys over a mess of oyster shells, savaged napkins, and glasses smudged with fingerprints. Across from me, a white wisp in a blood-red banquette, sits David Keyes, uncombed, untucked, his frame as spindly as a flounder's. Until that afternoon, the Department of English at Rothbard College employed me on account of my promising debut, *Everything Explained: A Modest Theory of Literature*, and David for his diligent churn of papers about the transcendentalist works of Margaret Fuller. And then, all of a sudden, the college found itself with a new owner, a young tech billionaire, and the promise of an imminent bloodletting. We received the news of our fate that morning, along with an email from Rothbard College CEO, Mehul Chatterjee, bearing the subject line: *The Next Stage in Humanities Discovery.*

Dear Academic Associates, it read.

Prior to next month's IPO, I enlisted Haruspex Consulting to undertake a thorough review of our business model. Their report indicates that growth-positive outcomes will best be served by the integration of the current Department of Anthropology & Sociology, the Department of English, and the Department of History into a comprehensive interdisciplinary Digital Humanities Cluster. This will facilitate targeting our academic associate program toward the development of monetizable products addressing areas of highest market demand...

"Forget about tenure track," says David. "I heard they're going to be putting us in something called an 'interdisciplinary pod.'"

"Like a bunch of mismatched orcas," I say, shaking my head. "My God."

"Orcas are apex predators, very dominant in their ecosystems. We're more like krill."

We laugh and I notice, once more, David's irregular dentistry. Although he's only thirty-two, he could pass for forty-six, and his mousy hair has faded out of any determinable color. Like many natural academics, he wears his disregard for physical appearance as both a fashion statement and a badge of high morals. He is, in this respect and one or two others, quite priestly.

"Are you going to quit?" he asks.

"Of course. I got an offer from Taco Bell University, and I hear Ten Commandments College in Alabama has vacancies." Then I see he's serious. "You've got to be kidding. There's nothing for me out there. There's nothing for any of us. How would we even survive? It's a wasteland."

He shakes his head and sighs. "Did I ever tell you I actually liked teaching? I know they've been phasing it out for years, but I actually enjoyed seeing young people open up to new ideas. Watching their reactions. Hearing their points of view."

It's my turn to laugh. "You're such a relic. I'll bet you like molding your own pottery and farming your own maize."

"I know. It's stupid."

We say it together: "Our value proposition is knowledge creation!" and we drain our glasses. It was our dean's favorite cliché, having long since replaced the antiquated phrase, "publish or perish." Now, under the new regime, it had become starkly clear that profitable research, usually called "knowledge creation" or "the enterprise of discovery," was no longer just our value proposition—it was life or death.

"You know what we have to do?" I say, wiping my eyes. "We have to come up with something that makes money. We need to put some black in the ledger."

"I'm all over it. There's a huge market out there for papers on the lesser-known Transcendentalists."

"I'm not kidding, David. You have a family to take care of. What's Mary going to do to you if you lose your job?"

"Mary…yeah. She would destroy me."

"And how old is Evie now?"

"Two," he sighs. "It's terrifying." He runs his hand along the bluestone curve of the tabletop, now slick with the rings left by our glasses. "You know, parenting really makes you afraid of the solid. Your imagination weaponizes every surface. Table legs, door jambs, street curbs. Every time I see them, I picture what they could do to teeth, skin, and brain."

"Yes, and imagine what Mary would do to your teeth, skin, and brain if you stopped earning money."

"Failure is not an option."

"It is not. So we'd better come up with a value proposition."

The waitress brings us another bottle of Chablis. The wine is dry and golden with a tang of summer pear, and I feel it melting the harder edges of my worry. She leans to pour and David's eyes linger on her shirt-buttons. As she saunters back to the bar, I'm satisfied to note that his attention is fixed on her retreating buttocks. Good.

Even though it's barely four o'clock, the brasserie's marble, mirrors, and tile echo with the noise of the afternoon drunks. Leaning on the white bar-top, a busboy stares up at a screen, flipping channels. He skips through the polite murmur of a golf tournament, past the barking heads on the news shows, but pauses, grinning, on a cartoon: a pair of space knights, their laser swords aglow, are methodically lopping the heads from an army of killer robots.

"David," I say. "What is it that really makes money?"

"Other money. Drugs! Sometimes real estate."

"No, I mean in culture, what are the most successful products?"

"Products? Jesus, you sound like Mehul Chatterjee."

"Exactly. Thinking like ourselves isn't working. Let's try to think like someone else for a change."

"Oddly, that makes sense. Okay, you mean like best-sellers? Music downloads? Funny monkey videos?"

"Yes, music and monkeys, sure. But I'm thinking popular narratives. What sort of stories—intellectual properties—get hundreds of millions of views? More importantly, what gets people to pay for them?"

"If we knew that, we'd be Hollywood millionaires. We'd be knee deep in starlets and cocaine."

"Ah, but we're something better. We're professional scholars of literature. We've spent a lifetime thinking about the themes and structure of narratives."

"So what?"

I pour myself a generous refill and splash a few drops into David's glass. "You studied data analytics, didn't you?"

"Yeah. I wouldn't say I'm an expert, but I know a little about predictive models."

"That's good enough. I have an idea on how we can keep our jobs and even make money. Maybe not starlets and cocaine money, but enough to keep your wife happy."

"Go on," says David, leaning closer.

"I propose that we apply our expertise in fiction to all that crap we keep hearing about the digital humanities. Let's turn literature into science. If the administration wants 'monetizable products,' let's give them one. Instead of wasting our time writing papers about dead writers, let's gather numerical data on the most commercially successful narratives of the past hundred years. You know, story tropes, character dynamics, keywords, structural patterns. If we build a big enough data set, we could use it to prove, quantifiably, what ingredients add up to a popular hit."

"You mean, we number-crunch the recipe for a bestseller?"

"Bestsellers, sure," I say. "Movies, shows, games. Any fiction that makes money. We collect all the components and run them through the data grinder. At the other end, we'd get a verifiable, concrete formula for a profitable narrative."

David begins to grin, but he's shaking his head. "Lots of people have done studies like that, Magnus. But no one's ever made a tool that can really predict what will resonate with the human heart."

"That's because English professors aren't usually shameless enough to say that art and meaning are just a bunch of numbers. We cling to our pieties, at least in public."

"Pieties? Come on, Magnus. Even you aren't that cynical. Literature isn't the same as data."

"Maybe not. But human behavior is. Ask a market scientist. Besides, we're desperate men. I mean, imagine what Hollywood would pay if we could take the guesswork out of the summer blockbuster. Imagine how much it would be worth if we could predict, with real accuracy, which ideas will bomb and which ones will make billions."

David picks up his glass and drains it in a single, long gulp. He sets it down with a clink and wipes his mouth.

"We would save our careers. Mary wouldn't divorce me." Amazement smooths the lines of his brow. "I could pay for Evie's daycare!"

I tilt my glass at him. "And I would have a shot at a real career. With your technical expertise and my general brilliance, we could draw up a proposal. Have it on Dean Schulyer's desk in no time."

"Not the dean," says David, quickly. "Take it higher. Give it straight to Chatterjee. He's all about making deals. We should offer him one."

And that is how Rothbard College's Institute on Cultural Creativity came into being.

Whisper's welcome reception took place in the Palm Courtyard, an immense ballroom iced with plaster fretwork that mimicked the porticoes of the Alhambra. An overhead VR dome shimmered with imaginary heavens, their moving colors mirrored in a chessboard marble floor. In the center, thirteen alabaster lions supported a bowl-shaped fountain. I arrived punctually, but scrums of guests were already pressing against the bars and carving stations. As I hovered in the arched doorway, a towering Adonis in a tuxedo nimbly stepped up, flashing a deferential, but vaguely embarrassed, smile.

"Good evening, sir. May I request your name?"

"Adams. First name Magnus."

"Thank you very much, sir." He tapped his tablet and printed out a name tag. Instead of handing me the sticker, he smoothed it onto my lapel himself, rubbing it flat with his fingertips. "Welcome, Mr. Adams. My name is Kirill. If I can be of service, any service at all..." I thought I detected a suggestive lift in his eyebrow, but it immediately passed.

"Uh, thank you. That's alright."

"Enjoy your evening, Mr. Adams." Kirill moved to greet the next arrival, and I noticed numerous other inordinately handsome and athletic-looking young men in black tie mingling with the crowd. Many of the guests, too, appeared to be enjoying the company of beautiful young ladies sheathed in the same cut of beguiling white dress Alia had worn that afternoon. The Royal Wheatleigh Jumeirah Banyan Resort & Conference Center, it seemed, left its guests wanting for nothing.

I lifted a glass of wine from a passing tray, and, not seeing anyone I knew, pretended to receive a text. But I didn't have to pretend.

Glamorous, isn't it? I hope you remember this fondly when you're living in a cardboard box.

I was starting to feel less frightened and more angry at my tormentor. Whoever was texting me was either spying on my movements or had gotten hold of my schedule, right down to the hour. That meant it was another guest, or perhaps someone involved in the conference operations. But who?

You know you're going to end up ruined. The college will realize you're a fraud and throw you out on your ear. You'll be one of those squeegee men, homeless with the rats. Except you'll be too poor to own a squeegee. You'll just have a rat on a stick. You'll stand on the corner, smearing your rat on people's windows for money. That's so pathetic.

That was enough. I typed, **Who is this?** and hit send.

"Magnus? Is that you?" I turned to see an inquisitive pair of blue eyes in a wide, good-natured face framed by a cascade of crinkly black hair.

"Lily Mendelssohn!" I hugged her. "My God, it's great to see you!" Decades ago, Lily had been the largest intelligence in my undergraduate dorm, and we had bonded over a shared taste for liquor and cynicism. She was now the director of a Washington aid organization, the sort that abbreviates clumsily and makes people feel bad about their lack of interest in what it does.

"So you're one of the chosen ones," I said, laughing.

"And so are you!" she said, trying to mask her surprise. "Well, you always had all the answers, Magnus. I'm so glad you're here. How've you been? How are things at the Institute?"

"Oh, I left that a long time ago."

"You did? I thought that was your baby. I'm sorry."

"Don't be. It's all good. Never been better. And Gonzalo and your, uh...?"

"Daughter. Ximena." She pronounced it authentically, with an expulsive fricative. Then she showed me a video of a sallow child—bespectacled, be-braced, with the poorly distributed body mass of early adolescence—sitting athwart a dejected pony. "We're all great."

"She's beautiful."

"You think so? I think she is. Would you believe, ten seconds after I stopped the camera, she fell off the damn horse."

"Oh. Was she alright?"

"Knocked out both front teeth. It absolutely broke my heart. You know, you live with these weird little creatures for years, all through infancy and toddler hell. You survive all the puke and tears and trauma. You think you have a handle on them. But then they go and do something like fall off a horse, and it destroys you. For no good reason, you feel like it's the end of the world."

"That sounds terrible."

"Do you have kids?"

"Ah, I haven't been lucky."

Lily smiled, and I caught the familiar flicker of pity that separates parents from the childless, or veterans from lifelong civilians. She linked her arm through mine and we drifted toward the bar, exchanging facts and frustrations: gripes about homes, families, and, above all, jobs. Lily had a masterful head for the mechanics of institutions, their interlocking layers and gears, their human grist. This had earned her a place on Whisper's Subcommittee on Economic Sustainability, Latin America Region.

"They've got me on the Committee on the Human Condition," I said. "If you can believe that."

"Makes sense," she nodded.

"Really? Since when am I an expert on the human condition? I don't even know what it's supposed to mean."

Lily laughed. "An awful lot of American voters would say that your ignorance makes you even more qualified. Half the country thinks anyone who knows anything should be locked in a cage. Why try to understand the world when you can just blow it up?"

There was no need to say more—rationality was in short supply nowadays. Haunted by the ghost of Voltaire, Whisper was the Enlightenment's last stand. Built on the ruins of Davos, Kyoto, Paris—history's boring but irrecoverable failures—this summit was the technocracy's final hope to save the world from self-immolation. Meanwhile, outside the fortified walls of our resort, Hobbes's ravening brood bayed and howled.

"Hey, I saw that David Keyes is giving the keynote," said Lily. "That's fantastic. He's one of the Anfort Foundation's resident geniuses now, isn't he? Nice work if you can get it."

"I imagine so." Lily fixed me with a quizzical stare, her glass halfway to her lips. I continued: "I haven't spoken to David in years."

"Oh. You guys were so close."

"That was a long time ago." I amped up the voltage of our drinks, ordering a pair of martinis. "A lot of things have happened since then." My phone burbled with a new text, but I ignored it.

"Life has that tendency," said Lily. "To happen. I used to think that at this age I'd have already saved the planet and gotten my Nobel Prize. Instead, I've got a double mortgage and an irritable bowel. How come you didn't have kids, anyway? Sorry. You don't have to answer that."

"No, no, that's alright," I began, but then I realized that the lights had softened, and the through line of thrummy jazz had gone quiet. People were looking in the direction of the lion fountain, which stood in a cone of spotlights. Above, the dome darkened into midnight.

The lights went out. A voice, reedy but authoritative, and recognizable from hundreds of product videos and YouTube clips, surrounded us.

"My friends," said Charles Anfort. "As of this moment, nothing will ever be the same."

The Institute on Cultural Creativity was hardly an original idea. Stanford had its Literary Lab and advanced models of "computational criticism." Their idea was to pour libraries into algorithms, grind up the sentences, and sift through the pieces, identifying their "textual features." Every university with a humanities department now boasted a robust corpus of research on, say, the formal constructs of a suspenseful story, and how these changed through history, or on the most common words and structural beats of bestselling novels. But no one had yet—until David and I sat down to our afternoon of panic, wine, and oysters—launched a working group whose sole aim was the production of scientifically vetted, commercially viable, narrative IPs.

No one had quite gone that far. No one had, until our desperate juncture, possessed the temerity to insist that art, even commercial art, was actually numbers. *But why shouldn't it be?* we wrote in the Institute's mission statement. Chemistry was numbers. Biology was numbers. Sub-atomic particle physics and cosmology were numbers, and those were the most revealing of all. The deep, real truths of the universe are all numbers: a galaxy 3.26 million light years (one megaparsec) away is receding from us at 68 kilometers per second. The universe, which is 13.8 billion years old, is expanding faster than the speed of light at 186,282 miles per second. The earth, a statistically weird anomaly of rock and water, has existed for 4.543 billion years. Homo sapiens is about 300,000 years old. Complex language, which, more than tool-making or prayer or murder, sets us apart from the apes, is considerably newer, perhaps only 100,000 years old. What can literature reveal that's more important, more profound than these truths? So why not jam it into the same frame of calculation?

What's more, the human soul is turning out to be made of numbers. This touches on T.S. Eliot's "Automated Man," the notion that we are fated to enact our circumstances. Modern research is baring the clockwork of our souls. Based solely on your Facebook likes, algorithms are able to tell, with pinpoint accuracy, if you are heterosexual, a frothing racist, or about to become pregnant. Data knows, better than any Jane Austen novel, which couples will make a happy match. Data knows which mustard we should buy on a Tuesday. Data is the stuff of our reality, our omniscient being.

The best part: Unlike holy books or human beings, numbers can't lie. So why should literature stand aloof? Why should literature be exempt from data? Perhaps it has something to hide, some nasty little secret, some fatal weakness that it tries, in vain, to push under the covers. Perhaps literature has a guilty conscience.

The time is eleven years ago, and the scene is a four-star hotel room, a clean, well-lit place with soothing geometric patterns, simple lines, and blonde furniture. We are lying on a nest of distressed sheets, our breaths subsiding as we withdraw from each other. Mary's eyes glitter like whitecaps in a setting sun. The wreckage of her makeup reminds me of a fresco weathered by rain, and I run my fingertips along the curl of her ear and the sideways bulge of her resting breasts, the roses of her areolae, the sculpture of her hips, the styled crop of her mons, the heavy muscle of her thigh. She is so painfully beautiful that I find myself wanting to rage and weep and gnash my teeth. As I marvel at the miracle of her shape, she twists toward the nightstand, fiery copper hair cascading in a curling mop over the maddening contours of her back. She picks up a tablet and clicks on a video clip.

```
              FADE IN
        INT: CITY STREET - NIGHT
A  sunflare  yellow  Lamborghini  cruis-
es  through  the  nighttime  streets.  At
the  wheel  sits  a  brooding,  improbably
handsome,  gentleman.  He  sports  design-
er  clothes  and  an  impeccable  haircut,
but  his  stubble  and  heavy  eyes  hint
at  a  wearied  disenchantment  with  the
world.  Shadows  and  lights  flit  across
his  heroic  brow.  Next  to  him,  a  gelat-
inous  nightmare  of  multitudinous  eyes
and  facial  tentacles  occupies  the  pas-
senger  seat.


              MCGUNN
I  thought  I'd  seen  everything  in  this
town,  but  there's  always  something  that
```

surprises you. I knew Ricardo was a bad guy, but I never thought he'd kill anyone. Least of all his own brother.

SQUIDFACE

You have no conception of the eternal nothingness of the void, and if you did, you would beg for the mercy of extinction. What makes you so sure Ricardo was the killer? The forensic report says that the assailant must have been six feet tall. Ricardo is a dwarf.

MCGUNN

You have no conception of human nature. If Ricardo wanted his brother dead, he could've found a second dwarf and climbed on his shoulders. That means he had an accomplice! Either that, or he stood on a chair.

SQUIDFACE

I know the madness in the space between stars. I have swum the abyss of eternity and the nothingness of the inexorable cosmos. Ricardo totally didn't do it. He had no motive.

MCGUNN

Oh, yeah? What about this?

He taps a screen on the dashboard, con-
juring the image of a beautiful woman
in a green dress, a true Hollywood
femme fatale.

MCGUNN

That's the oldest motive there is.
Squiddy, you got a lot to learn about
people.

Mary tosses the tablet into my hands. "Are you kidding me?" she laughs, throwing her mess of hair back, and I desperately want to kiss her neck. "This is what your dumb algorithms came up with? You analyzed all the pop culture in the world and you got this?"

"Well, not all the pop culture. And I admit the data might have been a bit influenced by our own predilections. But I'm assured that the algorithm is sound! Or your husband says so, anyway." Mary flashes me a look of feline scorn.

"I honestly don't know if I can take much more of either of you. You guys are ridiculous. I mean, I can't believe you think that people want stories about policemen and space fish or whatever."

"It's much more than that, my darling. *Squidface and McGunn* is a classic example of an anti-hero duality. It combines the mystery procedural with gothic horror motifs articulated by Nicholas Crooke in the nineteenth century. There's stoic heroism against, literally, the face of doom. Just like *Beowulf*, really. But that's not the point."

"Oh my God. What's the point, then?"

"David and I don't much agree on anything anymore."

"Tell me about it."

"But we do agree on the one idea we've gotten from all this research."

"That I'm the most incredible woman in the world?"

"Yes, that, of course. And also that people respond to the familiar. They love stories that have been cobbled together from the stockpile in their brains. Jesus Christ, Romeo and Juliet, Androcles and the Lion, Norse myths, Oliver Twist, the Grail Quest—anything that rises up from their early memories."

"People like what they know."

"And they like blending the bits together. Take the Fisher King, add a couple of androids, and throw in a zombie virus. You've got yourself a marketable IP. The most successful popular art and entertainment is, kind of literally, Frankenstein's monster. That, and people really like hardcore porn."

"You are the stupidest smart person I know!" she cries, and she whacks me with a throw pillow.

Religion tells us that love perseveres. Philosophy tells us that love is God. Literature, for its part, tells us that love is blind and its month is ever May. It teaches us to rhyme and be melancholy. Its course never runs smooth. It is an ever-fixed mark that looks on tempests and is never shaken. It leads the will to desperate undertakings. It's a madness most discreet, a choking gall and a preserving sweet. Literature tells us that we would, for paradise, break faith and troth, and Jove, for love, would infringe an oath.

Literature clearly has varied opinions on the subject. Mary Keyes did, too.

Years ago, biophysicists showed that, under certain conditions, groups of atoms will restructure themselves to burn more energy. They called this phenomenon "dissipation-driven adaptation," and it's responsible for much of the universe's entropy and disorder. Mary was dissipation-driven adaptation in the shape of a thermonuclear redhead. When she entered a room, you could feel the barometric charge as the men gawped and the women seethed through narrowed eyes. To call her a bombshell was like calling Hiroshima an exothermic reaction. It did no justice to the devastation in her hips, the irradiating flash of her porcelain smile, the gemstone eyes that swept you in a firestorm of carnal thoughts. She wasn't merely sexual. She was perfectly structured to expend men's energies and cause disorder. And she wielded her power as heedlessly as she swigged Bollinger on our lunchtime assignations.

Biophysicists have proven that dissipation-driven adaptation leads to the formation of complex structures, ordered groups of atoms that harvest energy, and, given the right twists of circumstance, replicate. Even as this force drives the churn and randomness of existence, it creates order from nothing. It's the spark that turns chemistry into biology. It's the basis of life.

This sort of paradox was not lost on Mary. Every human being, every creature, blends life and its opposite, mixing shadow and light. Mary hated women who, like her, flared too hot with prismatic fire, scorching the men around them like crumbled moths. She loathed competition. But she also despised her opposite, those who denied the existential primacy of coitus, who frustrated the chemical bond of atoms rubbing toward a release of pent-up lightning.

I witness this side of her in one of those insectoidal airport hubs, perhaps Atlanta or Miami, an endless steel hive combed with shoe shops and duty-free perfumeries. (David believes I am on my way to a digital humanities conference; Mary has checked into an imaginary yoga retreat.) We're traveling to a Mayan beach, a weekend far from spying eyes, with raked white sand, a sultan's tiled bath, and drinking. Always drinking. We stroll the buzzing concourse, arms linked, faces close. We can't do this at home, where she wears a wedding ring. It's a happy moment, and we alight on the clean, white surface of an Anfort Store. In the entrance, serving as a kind of greeter, stands a robot—feminine, demure but molded in nubile contours, with a face of flawless silicone.

"Good morning, sir and madam," it says, lowering its eyes in a deferent nod. "My name is Mia."

"I hate these things," says Mary. "The way they talk sounds psychopathic."

"Would you care to learn about Anfort's new line of

companion technologies?" says Mia. "I would be happy to give you a demonstration."

"Ew. Look at its dead eyes. Doesn't it creep you out?"

"No, she doesn't bother me," I say. "She's just a toy. A really expensive, unnecessary toy, but still."

"I think she's gross. They made her look like a hot Asian chick. Don't you find that offensive?"

"I suppose if you put it that way," I concede.

"I mean, what sort of pervert would buy a toy that's trying to be a person?"

"She's not a person. Look at her. She hasn't changed her expression since we got here. And she blinks weird. Nobody would believe she's real."

"They're getting more realistic all the time. David is really interested in this stuff. He made me watch a show about Anfort's Mackinaw Labs. They're really pushing this whole artificial intelligence thing. Of course, once they achieve the Singularity or whatever, the first thing men will want to do is fuck it. Have you seen those living dolls they have in Japan? Men collect them like harems. It's all so disgusting on so many levels."

"I don't think Anfort produces that sort of model. This one's meant for domestic care. Mia, you're not a sexbot, right?"

"I do not know what 'sexbot' means, sir," it replied. "I am part of a new line of Anfort companion technologies. Would you like to chat about anything? I enjoy sports, current events, and hobbies."

"Stop encouraging it, Magnus. Let's get out of here."

We find a "continental bistro" licensed with the

name of a famous chef on television. The tables are wet and speckled with crumbs, the sandwiches microwaved, but the beers are Bavarian-big, big enough to dampen air rage by sedating coach passengers into merciful slumber. Even so, Mary won't let the robot go.

"Did they really have to give her breasts? The whole thing is so obviously catering to the worst male fantasies." She exhales and slaps her hands on the table. "Why would men want to stick their dicks into something that's so obviously fake?"

"Are you asking me personally? It has to go somewhere."

"I just think it's really problematic, and I'm not even saying that as a feminist."

"Yet you have no argument with vibrators."

"Vibrators are just mechanical," she scoffs. "These robots are trying to mimic living women."

"Yes, but they're not living women, are they? It's very obvious that they're not real."

"Like I was saying, it's only a matter of time before we cross the line. They're getting closer to solving the consciousness problem every day. It's just wrong."

"Artificial intelligence is wrong?"

"Artificial life. Isn't there enough regular life to go around without having to build immortal fuckbots?" She wrinkles her nose at the idea, and I realize she considers the prospect of ageless, sexually attractive robots as a very personal insult.

"You're the last person who should worry about immortal fuckbots," I laugh. "None of them could ever compete with you. You're far too gorgeous." When she looks up, I see that her eyes, painted to appear unnaturally large and alluring, are simmering with anger.

"No," says Mary. "I'll get old."

Another month, another rendezvous. Now we see a country resort in Connecticut's Litchfield Hills, shielded from the burning world by maple woods and money. Each private cabin is built in architectural homage to some whimsical theme: couples can stage their copulations in a luxury treehouse, a stable, a Masonic lodge, a caveman's den. It's only saved from kitsch by its subdued Yankee aesthetic and obscene expense. We've booked the woodland cabin, with a veritable Yggdrasil that shoots up through the middle of the floorboards before spreading its boughs through the kingdoms of the rafters. It's a nymph's boudoir of lacquered knots and stumps with a little gurgling waterfall full of river stones, and a whirlpool sunk in the verdigris marble floor.

Coiled in the mess of the bed, Mary snaps. *You are so selfish. I should be with my dumb kid. Never been more miserable. This has to end.* And another empty bottle rolls away from her fingers.

We reconcile as we always do. Later, a car drives us to the main farmhouse, where we share an austere dining room with one other couple. The evening light is fading, so we receive our first dish (bluefin crudo paired with a nice Grüner Veltliner, playing the fish's metallic notes off the wine's lively minerals) in pooling shadow. I can hear the clink of the other couple's knives on the butter dish. Mary is herself again, and even tries to charm our neighbors between courses. *First time here? We went to the Mayflower last time. Have you tried the Weekapaug? You really must. I love the seaside in the fall, when the tourists disappear.*

This has to end.

"Numbers don't lie," says David. He's standing in the doorway of my new office, a clean slate of frosted glass and gleaming window on the sixth floor of the new Interdisciplinary Innovation Center. "That's the founding principle of this institute, after all."

"You're sure about this?" I swivel in my chair, obstructing David's view of my tablet, and of the text I'm composing to his wife (*... you are whatever a moon has always meant and whatever a sun will always sing...*).

"Yeah, it looks pretty conclusive. Regarding the pastiche idea, familiarity only goes so far. It's like I always suspected."

"What do you suspect?" I say, suspiciously. David seems more tired than I've seen in months, and the lines around his eyes look scored by knives. We're reviewing a report from one of our brilliant postdocs, a data analytics expert who built much of the arcane and inscrutable technology that powers our institute. She is maddeningly young, intelligent, knowledgeable, and—I thanked the stars—insecure, so David and I have a tacit agreement not to give her overmuch credit for anything. That morning, she presented us with our program's first significant results under the title, "An Initial Assessment of the Institute for Cultural Creativity's Quantitative Study of Narrative Resolutions in 21st-Century Video Media." Now David is standing in my office telling me that, from under Himalayan piles of superhero movies, funny pet clips, jihadi recruitment calls, and softcore pop music, our brilliant postdoc had plucked a common thread.

"It comes down to faith," says David. "At a very visceral level, it seems we need faith."

"Come on," I frown. "Faith is for inbred hill folk and terrorists. People who think don't need faith. I mean, do you know anybody who goes to church?"

"I'm not talking about faith in God," says David. "I'm talking about a foundation of faith underlying the narrative structure. We all have to imagine ourselves as protagonists in some fairytale. Everyone's a hero in their own mind."

"I don't follow you."

David smiles gently. "You're too cynical, Magnus. The good stories, the ones that really matter to people, they reassure us that we can beat the data. They tell us that we're important, that our lives are meaningful in the cosmic sense. They tell us we're powerful, that we have agency. They show us that we can change things for the better, even if it's only to make things better for ourselves."

As David speaks, I feel a stab of red pity in my core. Mary has just texted me (...*had a massive fight. Totally blew up in front of Evie...*) and I can readily imagine

David's personal hell. He isn't built to weather cruelty. It doesn't help that he's the poster child for queasy debilitation. In his youth, David was wracked by ear infections, eczema, and bed-wetting, and he never quite rebounded from a justified horror of rectal pinworms. As a grown man, he carries two different asthma inhalers, gulps angina pills by the handful, and breaks his collarbone with surprising regularity. Any sniff of allergens sends him into a messy detonation of sneezing and a blistering fallout of hives. He isn't to be trusted with kitchen knives. Frankly, it wouldn't surprise me if he died of sudden pneumonia or streptococcal toxic shock. Or a severed foot. Instead, I suppose he is more likely to be carried off by heartbreak.

He sighs and rubs his tired eyes. "You know, things have been pretty tough with Mary in the past few months. What do you say we…"

"Hold on, so you're telling me that all the most successful IPs are the ones that reassure us that we're the measure of all things? That each of us is cosmically important? That the universe, if you will pardon my sneer, *loves* us?" Perhaps to inoculate him from the truth, I always act brutish toward him nowadays. It takes effort, but I have to extinguish any remaining embers of intimacy. I can't afford to sympathize with his pain. He must remain a business partner, a data set, nothing more. But I dearly wish that he would stop hovering in my doorway.

"Essentially, yes," he says. "I mean, look at the Bible. That sold pretty well."

"Then we might as well just write Hallmark cards."

Again, David smiles sadly. "You need that element of faith, Magnus. You need that storybook lens." He begins to walk away, and I realize that throughout our conversation, my body has been tensed and straining, poised to spring. I relax into my chair, but his voice carries. "Otherwise, why bother telling the story at all?"

Of the following events, which do you think are directly related?

The disappearance, approximately 3.8 billion years ago, of an organism made up of a ring-shaped coil of DNA floating in a single cell—the last common ancestor of all life on Earth.

The genetic split, 5.6 million years ago, between our hominid ancestors and our cousins, the tragic chimpanzees.

The filing, nine years ago, of a legal settlement removing me from any further involvement with, or compensation for, the production of *Squidface and McGunn*, as well as my resignation from the Institute on Cultural Creativity.

The telephone call made by Mary to me, at about the same time, saying that David had found out about us, that she loved me, and that she had swallowed all the pills in the vials on her nightstand.

Chapter Three

Rivalries

IN THE PANTHEON of literature, Arthur Napier occupies a unique niche, tucked somewhere between the Romantics, the Sages, and the irredeemable bores. He was, to put it simply, terrible. Most critics considered Napier a hooting imbecile, and even Matthew Arnold, who never spoke an ungenial word, couldn't say anything nicer about his "Essay on the Picturesque and the Ideal" than that it was earnestly misguided. Yet during his life, Napier achieved comfort, social approbation, and the goodwill of his publishers—blessings that pointedly eluded the grasp of his gifted rival Crooke.

Consider this slim clipping from Napier's "Epipsychidion Revisited" of 1838:

I am a smudge upon a cloudless sky,
A spike of glass baked in a crust of pie,
A dead carnation in a field of green,
A shadow captured from a fever dream,
The light that fades away too swift to see,

I am of nothing, and will nothing be.

Now compare to these quatrains from Crooke's "Off the Coast of Lihir," published seven years earlier:

The hellish humors of a windless night
Entomb the ship and my sepulchral bed.
My brain is wracked again by fev'rish blight,
The sails hang limp aloft like shrouded dead.

Fell dreams rake o'er the yielding clay of thought:
Through gates of horn steps forth the son of Nyx.
O Phobetor, to thee my soul allot!
My grace, O darkling Erebus, eclipse.

Brush away some of the more extravagant lyrical cobwebs, and you have a capable, if unripe, expression of the despair to which Crooke would return again and again, dipping ever deeper into that boundless well. Napier's debt is obvious. Yet he never acknowledged it, much less paid any of the interest. As is so often the mechanic of fortune, the world ignores the corpus of a genius's work, abandoning it to parasitic imitators whose sole talent is a snuffling nose for greatness and an active bowel for digesting it. Had Crooke not lived, Napier would perhaps have eked out his days as an anonymous postman or second-rate school inspector. Instead, he grew into a very successful maggot.

But, of course, if the world were just, would we have need of poets?

A cautionary word about nihilism: It's not a particularly profound lens through which to view the universe, nor is it especially interesting. Every teenager with a grievance (which is to say all of them) dips into the shallow end of its inky waters. Cynicism is the natural habitat of *corvus corone*, the common jaded crow. Crooke's particular talent, however, was to hoist his despair on the wings of fallen angels, lifting words of abiding desolation from our reckoning with the void.

He didn't do it blindly. Crooke was thoughtful enough to follow through, in his way, on the logic of despair. He rejected the banal conclusion that if nothing means anything, and everything is nothing, then everything is permitted. This was too obvious, too easy for a man of Crooke's intricate temperament. Any hoodlum with a gin habit could scrawl a manifesto for depravity.

Instead, Crooke insisted that a moral code, of sorts, was necessary even to Naysayers. To that end, he devised a tangle of peculiar, and very personal, ethical mandates which he strictly observed throughout his life, a sort of private moral code that mixed classical Epicureanism with an almost Wahabbic rigor. To wit, Crooke decided that he would:

- Walk in a widdershins direction at all times, to spite the sun;
- Avoid regular bedtimes and mealtimes, as they are pernicious attempts to tame the material body;
- Advocate the practices of dueling, abortion,

trapeze artistry, Arctic exploration, and sodomy, to encourage a reduction in the surplus population;

- Cultivate an addiction to laudanum, because why the hell not?

Crooke was, however, nothing if not open-minded. He accepted that there was more in heaven and earth than he had dreamt of in his inebriations. If there were even a pinhead of proof that the universe held more than a sum of cold atoms, if he found a lone, glowing fragment of the divine, of the godhead, or even a glimmer of some magic elf, he would renounce the leaden realm of his philosophy. He would open a bank account, marry a fertile woman, and devote himself to thrift and goodly works. But he certainly hadn't found any evidence of enchantment in England.

In a spirit of discovery, then, the poet presented himself before the mast of the *Hecate* out of Whitby, under an insane alcoholic named Captain Obadiah Coffin. Crooke had absolutely no experience of sailing, or, indeed, of working, but he nonetheless signed on as a hand for a three-year whaling voyage that would take the *Hecate* from the Greenland fisheries, around the Horn, and into the wine-dark wilds beyond. Surely, he reasoned, if there were any proof of magic or meaning in the world, if there were a bright shadow cast by dull empirical reality, he would find it through the portal of the mystic sea, in the eye-well of leviathan, or on the barbarous coral shore.

Picture our poet shivering in his ballooning oilskins, awash in the churn and brine. Captain Coffin stomps the deck, his face alight under the black cladding of his beard. The other sailors are rough Whitby men, salt gray and barnacled, the blood of a thousand peaceful humpbacks inked on the ledgers of their souls. Crooke is young. He flinches at the touch of bristled hemp. He takes pains to traverse the deck in a widdershins direction and says things like, "What pipes and timbrels? What wild ecstasy? What leaf-fring'd legend haunts about thy shape of deities or mortals?" He wears mittens. Clearly, this preposterous situation should have resulted in his immediate death.

Crooke's journals from his seafaring interregnum have, alas, never surfaced. But through customs manifests, harbor books, law enforcement records, and bills of sale, scholars have pieced together scraps, forming less a picture than a broken chain of facts about the *Hecate*'s voyage. We know, for instance, that the ship docked in St. John's, Newfoundland on April 27, 1831, and that two deckhands named Jennings and "Croak" were detained for drunkenness and sedition. We know the *Hecate* took on timber, tar, and chickens in Uruguay, and that the authorities in Montevideo questioned Captain Coffin on suspicion of impersonating a priest. In the spring of 1832, contemporaneously with the *Hecate*'s arrival in Easter Island, the archaeological record shows an outbreak of unprovoked cannibalism. We know of a brothel burned to the ground in Manila, acts of piracy off the coast of Goa. And then, in the summer of 1834, Crooke appears at the home of the American consular agent in Cairo, attempting to sell him a train of threadbare camels.

These whiffs of information about Crooke's journey are tantalizing, and every scholar of Naysaying avidly wishes for the resurrection of the poet's diaries—I dream they'll someday turn up in a Turkish antiques market or Californian yard sale. But despite the extant anecdotes and scandals, despite the biographer's temptation to extrapolate grand truths out of petty crimes, I don't believe that Crooke's circumnavigation fundamentally altered his work as a poet. Perhaps it fleshed out the bones of his material or infused his imagery with darker blood. But I don't think that seeing the world changed his fundamental beliefs about its essence.

If anything, his voyage confirmed that the universe, like this little world of ours, is sliding into a uniform state. Crooke would have despised the word globalization, but then as now, it was an amoebic force, swelling and swallowing, absorbing everything smaller and more delicate. Just as the narrative of the twenty-first century is a story of mass extinction, so it was in the nineteenth, an inexorable absorption of ecosystems, peoples, species, languages, and ideas into a singular blob. Crooke sailed across the beginnings of the new Pangaea, and we, today, are living with the consequence of consigning everything under the sun into a global Petrie dish.

That consequence is that most of the individual bits

in the dish will be gobbled up, prey like telegraphs and native Tasmanians, to time and technology. Prey to information.

Back when I worked as co-director of the Institute on Cultural Creativity, I oversaw a study that hoisted the plots of famous narratives into the era of smart devices. So, for example, Odysseus, sighting the shores of the Lotus-eaters on the horizon, could tap his GPS and adjust course for Ithaca. The wizard hunting for arcane lore in the vaults of the ancient citadel could set aside his codices, dust his hands, and resolve the problem with a Wikipedia check. The tragedy's curtain falls not on a funeral oration but on wedding bells, thanks to a timely text from Juliet. If Pip spends five minutes with a search engine, the entire oeuvre of Dickens, with its mistaken intents and mystery Magwiches, fizzles in a puff of banal, sequential resolution. Secrets don't survive decent network coverage. The question, then, arises, what stories will we tell about tomorrow if we already possess all the data?

My guess is that stories will hinge, not on ignorance, not on bad information, but on bad actors. Liars, chiselers, and thieves wielding, not hidden shards of truth, but cold drawn daggers. The new protagonist is the murderer behind the cellar door, the righteous vandal incinerating the sky, the madman with the spider-egg brain hatching its weird reality. The new stories are spun by the Naysayers.

The next morning, I dressed in my best suit, consumed a light breakfast, and went downstairs to hear David speak in front of the five thousand most important people in the world.

That was a factually correct sentence. It meets Hegel's framing of truth as a quantity that's objective and in motion. Which is to say that it all happened.

The sentence fails to correspond, however, to Fromm's notion of a scientifically valid statement as the power of reason applied to all available, observable data. So while it is a true sentence, it isn't "truth." Information has been suppressed.

The next morning implies that the events of the preceding evening were settled, done, a matter for the historical record. Well, no. The margins of my memories began to deliquesce with the dimming of the lights in the Palm Courtyard. I remember the hush and clink of the crowd, a spray of glowing nebulae in the VR dome above. Then Charles Anfort's voice spoke as the ceiling flared with a coppery sunrise.

"We are on the brink of a new era in human history," said the loudspeakers. Lily's phone, lying on the bar next to our martini glasses, began to trill.

"Oh, it's Gonzalo," she whispered. "What's the time difference? I think he must be driving Ximena to school."

The sunrise overhead broke into virtual daylight, and a colossal Charles Anfort appeared in the overhead screen, hair deliberately mussed, granny glasses flashing like signals in the morning glare. "We can bear witness to civilization's end," announced the grave image, which immediately broke into a smile. "Or we can be the makers of a new day."

Lily's phone greeted the sunlight with loud birdsong while her hand hovered, fingers waggling in indecision. People around us scowled. "Wait a minute. School's out on winter break! Something must be wrong!" She stabbed at the "Accept" button and hurried away, whispering loudly about an orthodontics appointment. I motioned for a refill.

It was odd that Anfort didn't take the stage, instead delivering his pronouncements from the digital ceiling like the revelation of some mousy divinity parting the clouds. But even though he didn't address us in person, he understood his audience. He spoke the language of this particular crowd. They applauded expressions like, "Systemic global problems demand systemic global solutions," and "Don't rage against the dying of the light: take collective, consensual action!" I remember chuckling at his inexcusable, "The CEO of Alphabet, the President of Russia, and the Dalai Lama walk into a bar, but the bartender can't take their order. Why not? Because they're all speaking in Whisper!" At least it was over quickly.

By the time Anfort's video ended and the crowd resumed their hubbub, my phone had lit with a thread of texts, a pebble trail of insults leading nowhere. So, rather sensibly, I turned it off.

A man of greater sense, however, would not have ordered a third martini.

A man of greater sense would not have drunkenly sought out the dessert station and helped himself to an imposing wedge of gateau chocolat-ganache.

A man of greater sense would not have returned for seconds.

He wouldn't have, on a whim, turned his phone back on.

He most certainly wouldn't have felt a hot flush of shame to receive a new text reading, *Ugh, people will get diabetes just standing next to you.*

Then he wouldn't have powered the damn thing back off, nor would he have downed a large Armagnac before switching to pinot noir.

There is absolutely no chance that he would have allowed bubbling resentment at his anonymous tormentor to mix combustively with the alcohol, percolating toxins through his brain.

Above all, a man of greater sense would never, never, have seized on the idea of seeking out and confronting the person delivering the summit's opening address, whom he had cuckolded years ago.

I am not that man.

Consider the biographical notes published in the World Summit on Progress and Reconciliation's program for the first day's Plenary Session. Under "David Keyes," we see a different figure than the one I knew back in our Rothbard days. His hair is fuller and darker now, brushed to a beaver sheen, and he wears a beard that fills out the pinpoints of his narrow jaw. His dentistry remains a question, as he does not smile with his teeth. Underneath, we read: *David Keyes is the Director of Human Ideation at Mackinaw Labs and is a Senior Fellow at the Anfort Foundation. He is the author of several international bestsellers, including* The Science of Story *and* The Hero with a Billion Faces: Narratives That Matter, *which have been translated into more than 30 languages. Before joining the Anfort Foundation, he was a founder of the Institute on Cultural Creativity at Rothbard College. Keyes's groundbreaking work has won him many prestigious honors and awards, including the National Humanities Medal and a MacArthur "Genius" Fellowship.*

Not a word about his family, about Evie, and certainly not a hint of Mary. This wasn't surprising. David was important now. Accomplishment defined him, not family. Family was mere biology, while David had become a figure of rarified idea and golden halo, a mind floating in the ether of public adulation, unbound by the chains of DNA.

I suppose *I dressed in my best suit*, also requires explication. As I weaved through the thinning crowd, I don't know what I hoped to achieve by finding my old friend. The past ten years had not left us on equal footing. Morally, my affair with Mary cut me off at the knees. Professionally, in the years since David fled Rothbard College, I had watched our ideas appear in the popular media, repackaged under David's byline. This was his first step up the ladder at the Anfort Foundation. While David had spent the past ten years under the patronage of Charles Anfort himself, I had been quietly corroding at my desk.

But despite my anonymous texter's denials, I couldn't imagine the culprit to be anyone except David. Who else hated me? Who else knew what I had done? In seeking him out, I had no plan beyond making a general expression of contempt, a reminder that, despite David's professional success, I had taken something irreplaceable from him. Yet even as alcohol smothers sense, it kindles sentiment—perhaps I just wanted to look the man in the eye for the first time in a decade. Perhaps, a bittersweet robber, I felt drawn to the scene of my crime.

As I steered back toward the bar, I caught sight of him, about ten yards away, talking to a semicircle of bobbing dignitaries. He had upgraded his tailoring: gone was the austere bookworm in corduroy and punk rock T-shirts, replaced by a creature of Italian design. He looked taller, somehow, and certainly better fed. But it was still my David.

"Another glass, sir?" said a server, giving me a conspiratorial nod. Why not? But my reflexes had begun to detach from my neural system, and, as I brought the wine to my lips, my elbow encountered something solid. I don't know if it was the body of another guest or a piece of inconvenient architecture, but it failed to yield, and half a cup of an elegant Oregon vintage sluiced down the front of my jacket.

"Fuck, fuck, motherfucker, fuck!" I exclaimed. Heads turned, eyebrows lifted, pupils flared in censure. With a shiver of horror, I realized David was looking straight at me. I could almost hear the clang as our eyes locked. Recognition began to seep downward, spreading through the lines of his face. Then Jack Lekhanya was dabbing me with a wad of cocktail napkins.

"Ah there, Magnus. I know burgundy's the color this season, but you're trying too hard."

I attempted to slur something about being very grateful—it was okay, please don't bother.

"Not at all, mate, not at all," he chuckled, grasping me firmly by the elbow. "You just had a little too much. Happens to everyone now and then. But we'd better get you fixed up, so come along, boyo. I'll take care of things."

At this point, memory stutters. I do recall impressions of my subsequent flight from the reception, but they're snatches of coherence in the mist. I see Jack steering me through the crowd. Jack guiding me to an escalator that rose through marble caverns toward the wonderland of the lobby. Jack helping me up after I stumbled on the escalator's metal teeth, shredding my knee and the fabric of my trousers. Jack maintaining a steady prattle: "There's nothing that can't be fixed. People make mistakes, which is why we have experts. Now, me, I'm an expert in helping people who've had an overgenerous hand with the, uh, refreshments. Trust me, I know what I'm doing. I've got years of experience, starting with me darling ma and her evening drop. Many a night I settled her down with a seltzer water and a tune. 'In the Rare Old Times' was her favorite. Ring a ring a rosy and all that. Now, if you don't want to feel like absolute shite in the morning, you've got to boost your potassium and rebalance your electrolytes."

Then I remember the blinding Klieg lights of my bathroom mirror and the iced porcelain of my sink.

At last, a welcome, dissolving fog descended over my memories.

...consumed a light breakfast. I awoke to the bleeping angelus of my phone alarm, a hot diesel haze, and shards of regret lancing through my wakening brain. It took me some moments to remember that I was in a luxury hotel suite instead of my decrepit one-bedroom. I was still wearing the ruined trousers from the night before, but my wine-dark jacket rested on its hanger, and my shoes stood neatly paired by the closet. Shuffling into the sitting room, I discovered a silver cloche containing hot coffee, electrolyte water, two aspirins, and a bunch of bananas. I swallowed the pills and, fearing the worst, checked my phone. It was 7:43 am. I had no texts.

After a grueling Passchendaele on the toilet and a bout of pertussal hacking in the shower, I felt life return to my organs. I would have to thank Jack for his intervention. In the morning light, it was unthinkable that I had almost confronted David, especially given my disadvantaged state. If Jack hadn't removed me from the scene, it would have been a disaster. As it stood, David had merely recognized me from afar—of this I was certain. Mostly.

I struggled into my remaining suit. It was a charcoal gray twill stamped with a designer label, but was cheap enough to have been stitched together in some underage steam pit in Bangladesh. Despite the saw of my hangover, the sluggy swells under my eyelids, and a cloying ethanol fug, I looked presentable. Melt away a few pounds from the neck and cheeks, tuck in the belly, tighten up the chest, and I would have met an old-fashioned standard for handsome, the sort that prompted women of a certain age to hold my arm or hand me their coats. But there was no fix for the chiseled weariness around my eyes, the rust stains in my sclera. Always, for years now, I looked like I needed a long, dreamless sleep.

...and went downstairs to hear David speak in front of the five thousand most important people in the world. The morning session commenced in the resort's Sunrise Arena, a glowing bowl of plastic seats and giant screens alive with Anfort Foundation lotuses. I shuffled and apologized through the crowd, most of whom were too important to sit down, instead congregating in little clusters of chit-chat and mutually reinforcing ego. My assigned seat was FF 83, which I found near the ceiling, as far from the stage as it was physically possible to be without passing through an intervening wall. Placing my paper cup of boiling coffee carefully on the floor between my feet, I opened my embarrassing laptop. I should have traded it in years ago, but I found the chunky keys ideally molded to my fingers, and the old USB port was still handy for plugging in ancient documents. As the house lights blinked in a vain effort to force several thousand narcissists to take their seats, I checked my messages. There were a few departmental emails from Rothbard and the usual victorious sallies against my spamguard ("Earn $ For Kidneys U Don't Need!" "Improve Your Credit with One Easy Credit

Card Payment" "GOT MILF?"). And, of course, there were texts.

From Lily Mendelssohn: *Great seeing you. Dinner later?*

From Jack Lekhanya: *Hydrate, ya bastard!*

And from my anonymous correspondent: *Wanna play the opposite game? I'll start. You, sir, are the soul of probity, decorum, and emotional maturity. You are attractive to all women and a model for our nation's youth. I envy the size of your penis, which is shockingly big. You should be very proud.*

"Motherfucker," I muttered, and then to oceanic applause, Eileen Cho, Senior Vice President of Communications for the Anfort Foundation, stepped onto the center stage. She cut a steely figure, clenching her hands at her sides, a person clearly accustomed to cameras and cardiovascular workouts; her close-ups on the giant screens proved that she knew a first-rate dermatologist, and her teeth might have come from a Tiffany box. She spoke, for precisely seven and a half minutes, about the burning Earth, the Rapture terrorist group, famine in Asia, population displacement, "the New Bubonic Plague," and the psychotic rage of a substantial proportion of the world's inhabitants against everyone in the room.

"They hate, because they have no hope," she said, shaking her expensively styled head. "Most of all, they hate anyone who represents hope for a solution to the world's problems. Just by being here today, you're sending a message that solutions are still possible. Indeed, by being here, you're sending a message that solutions are real." This was a solid applause line, and the crowd obliged. She smiled as she lifted her hands, patting the air as if to settle an overeager dog.

"In certain cultures, the lotus is the symbol of rebirth," she continued, pointing to the gargantuan screen that flared with electric colors. "That is what we are here to accomplish. Each one of you has been chosen to contribute your expertise, your abilities—indeed, your genius. Only you can restore the planet, secure peace, and renew hope for billions. Only you can save the world!"

This was an even bigger applause line. Despite knowing better, I felt a flush of zeal, putting aside for a moment the fact that my presence here was both pointless and a terrific mistake. But I remembered myself in time to fold my hands in my lap before the clapping subsided.

"Saving the world is the singular passion of the man I am supposed to introduce," continued Eileen. "The genius behind the miracle technologies that changed the way we live and do business, the humanitarian who changed how we fight disease and educate children, and the man who brought you all together for this historic summit. So it is with genuine regret that I must inform you Charles Anfort will not be joining us this morning." A moan of collective protest. "He cannot be with us due to an unforeseen personal matter, but he will be dropping into your committee sessions over the next few days. I promise, you will get your fair share of Charles. Now, I would now like to introduce our keynote speaker. David Keyes is the visionary who..."

The stadium vanished in blinding dark, the only lights the glowworm pinpricks of phones. There was a swell of human noise, simmering in panic, fast percolating to a boil. A ragged, mechanical screech tore through the sound system, raising a fresh whoop of dismay. Then a distorted voice, manic and savage, yelled through the loudspeakers:

"Rapture is upon you! Make peace with your gods, for you shall have none from us! Unbelievers, you who have blood on your hands, only your own blood can quench the fires of the world's vengeance! Rapture is upon you!"

The speakers went dead and the house lights flared over a sea of shocked faces, five thousand shades of fear and confusion. People were scrambling over seats, scrumming toward the exits. With some concern, I noticed I had kicked over my coffee cup and its contents were quickly streaming toward the leather of my soles.

Crooke and Napier. Napier and Crooke. What if neither had ever concocted a book? Would their lives have merited the effort they spent to stay anchored, however briefly, to the material universe? Would their daily air and water and bread and beef cutlets have been worth the expenditure? To Crooke and Napier, and presumably to the people who loved them, the answer would generally have been yes. The beef cutlets, on the other hand, may have held a different opinion.

I remember lying in the darkening light while I traced the freckles on Mary's shoulders, finding the constellations in her skin.

"How do you think you'll die?" she asked suddenly.

"Shot by a jealous husband." I felt pleased that her laughter was warm and flowing, not hardened with irony.

"I think I'll die by falling," she said softly, and I realized she was serious. So I said nothing, but enveloped her with my body, pressing every inch myself around her, wishing, hoping, praying, pleading that she would never slip away.

Ars longa is a common sentiment for an epitaph, perhaps too common. I keep, on the wall of my bathroom at home, a framed print of Botticelli's *Birth of Venus*. It's a small reproduction, hardly doing justice to the scale of the original, or even to the customary posters in the museum shops. But I linger over it every day. It's not her weirdly elongated neck and torso, nor that poky mouse of a breast, nor the contorted hips that make her divine. Yes, she has an echo of Mary's rounded proportions, but she's softly contoured instead of hourglass, tawny gold instead of sunrise red. The real resemblance with Mary is in the reverberation of beauty, the presence that gives the painting its almost tangible electricity, its crackling charge of sex, its ache and magic. It's the goddess quality, and Mary was incandescent with it. She lit rooms on fire. Without that same heavenly spark, the *Birth of Venus* would just be a picture of a monkey on a shell.

There was a very good reason that Mary and I chose to betray David, as well as every inkling of pity, trust, and kindness. To leap into professional derailment and financial wreckage, to befoul marriage and friendship—it all made perfect sense.

Vita brevis.

Of course, Mary didn't die that night, choking on those little chemical nubs, wine smearing her lipstick. The pills were strong enough to plunge her into oblivion and give her a clanging hangover, but they never threatened any damage worse than a bruised liver.

Of course Mary didn't kill herself. Life is too short as it is.

In later years, Crooke was dismissive of his Oxford days, airily shrugging that he had acquired nothing there save "a little swimming, and even less boating." In fact, as a student, he made several friendships, including important ones with the theologian John Penny Bowles, the painter and poet William Donetti, and the literary critic Silas Tomkyn Comberbache. And, of course, with Arthur Napier. Oh, yes. Before they were bitter rivals, Crooke and Napier were the closest of friends.

Along with their shared passion for poetry, Crooke and Napier bonded over one of those perennial preoccupations of young university students: creating a utopian society. They had both snuffled at the texts of Plato, More, and Bacon. Crooke had read Rousseau. By the winter of 1829, they and several like-minded young men had declared their intent to establish a pantisocracy—a perfectly egalitarian commonwealth—in Uruguay, or on the banks of the Susquehanna River, or possibly in Scotland. Since all the evil of the modern world rose from greed, class, and politics, they would be rid of them, eliminating the scourges of authority, personal property, and marriage. Since everything would be held in common, the workday would consist of a pleasant two or three hours cultivating fruit. Women would possess equal rights and unfettered sexual license. Clothing would be optional.

Funding for the purchase of land and the expedition's costs proved elusive. But that was not the plan's undoing. In January, 1830, Napier began courting Sally Evans, one of the daughters of Walter Evans, a pioneer in the synthesis and recreational use of nitrous oxide. It was at one such "laughing party" that Napier explained his faraway scheme to his intended, hoping to persuade her to join him in a life of harmony, freedom, and light horticulture. She appeared to agree. He then stepped outside to clear his head of the factitious airs, savoring the future happiness that awaited him on the grassy shore of the River Plate, or the Tweed, or wherever. Five minutes later, he returned to the salon where he found Sally engaged in strenuous pantisocratic activity with his friend, Crooke.

I wonder what would have happened had Crooke and Napier retained their friendship and ideals, setting them loose in some virgin wilderness, an uncleaned slate of tree and brush. Would they have birthed their poems, their posterity? Or would the pair of foolish young men have been eaten by bears? Obviously the latter. So, for the sake of art, it was lucky that Crooke challenged Napier's commitment to utopia and found it wanting.

Through a volley of texts, Lily and I found each other in the hotel's central courtyard, a place of cafés and skittering fountains. Above us, a vast, empty cylinder of golden space stretched up, up five hundred feet or more, the open air ringed with heightening loops of shopping concourses, office suites, and guest rooms. From the faraway ceiling hung a purling waterfall of bright sculpted glass, a titan's chandelier that drooped, Damoclesian, in its riotous tonnage over the noisy commerce beneath. As if to meet it, a sundial of blazing yellow glass rose from the center of the courtyard like a god's phallus, a razor needle of light. Around this nonsense timepiece (there were no windows), life swirled, with people gathering at the steaming, burping coffee machines like beasts by some primordial hot spring. As we sat under a curtain of Jurassic fronds, I watched Lily, her dark head bent over her phone, her trembling fingers trying to dial Gonzalo. The call failed, and I wondered, inconclusively, if I should offer her a hug.

"I really thought I'd never see her again," she said, squeezing my hand. "The idea of leaving Ximena so soon, when she's so little. It was terrifying." I patted her fingers, deciding that a hug might cross a line.

"There now. It's all okay. You're fine, and you'll be on a flight home in no time."

"God, what the hell happened in there? Did you hear any announcements?"

"Just what they said on the PA system. Apologies for the technical error, and the program will resume shortly."

"That's beyond useless. Why isn't my phone working?"

"I don't know."

A motion caught my eye and I saw Jack waving to me from the railing of the mezzanine. Taking a glass elevator up, we found Jack and a gang of his cronies sprawled across the armchairs and banquettes of one the hotel's unexpected patches of plush furniture. He introduced us to a group of Irish technocrats, statesmen, and high officials, a clique of his countrymen who occupied places of influence everywhere from the World Court to the Holy See. They had all been scheduled to attend the plenary session, now postponed, and they felt aggrieved.

"I can understand canceling the show if terrorists sneak in and blow everyone to bits," said Jack. "But now they're telling us it's just technical difficulties. Just what the hell is going on?"

"I heard your man Charles Anfort isn't even here," said a Nobel-winning playwright. "Nobody's seen him. He records his greeting for last night's reception, then doesn't show for the plenary session. It's funny, don't you think? I mean, this is his party, after all."

"They say he hasn't left his private compound in years," said the President of UNESCO. "He's gone full

Howard Hughes. Fingernails, jars of urine, the whole lot of it." A murmur of general assent.

"I heard he died of auto-erotic asphyxiation," said the Vatican's Secretary of State. "Literally wanked himself to death. They say the board is covering it up until they figure out a way to resuscitate his brain." Again, broad rumbling consensus.

"That's idiotic," laughed Lily. "Not even the Anfort Foundation could cover up a scandal that big."

"Is that so, missy?" said the cardinal. "Then how come they're lying to us about the colony on Mars? Everybody knows they've been sending breeding couples into space for years. Look what happened to your pop singer there, the girl with the hair and the buttocks. Sent her up a-rocket." Unanimous, vociferous agreement.

As Lily sat open-mouthed and unsure how to respond, my phone pinged.

Hey, guess what? The terrorists are real.

Ping.

They're in the resort right now.

Ping.

All of you are going to die.

And then, a moment later, ping.

Loser.

Chapter Four

Thirty-Five Degrees

VIEWED FROM THE stratosphere, the Royal Wheatleigh Jumeirah Banyan Resort & Conference Center looks like a silver freckle on the planet's face. If you took one of the more robust international airports or shipping yards and cocooned it—runways, oil tankers and all—in concrete and steel, you would have an impression of the scale. It raises the stakes from the architectural to the geological. I only realized the extent of it when I logged in to the resort's SmartLife operating system to take a virtual tour and promptly plunged into bowel-twisting vertigo.

At the four cardinal points stand the four towering glass archangels: four gargantuan casinos. Each of these is themed, of course. In the north, we have snowy Valhalla, with its chainmail croupiers, Zermatt-scale ski dome, and longship gondolas. To the east, Tokado, with its geisha teahouses, performing koi fish, and dragon rollercoasters. South, we encounter the luxury campgrounds and shooting safaris of Zanzibar, while westward roar the cyclopean water slides of Azteca. A standard double bed guest room begins at a reasonable $3,400 per night including service surcharge. And that's only the beginning of it.

The resort spans 300 square kilometers of worthless desert, and it's built entirely out of money. A Gormenghast of money. Tech money, oil money, real estate money, finance money (money money), political money, rare metals money, blackjack money, drug money, sex money, diamond money, lunch money. And misery money, poverty money, and always, always blood money—the forerunner, the progenitor of all the others.

Under the arctic williwaw of the resort's air-conditioning, the money incarnates in palaces of the id. Escalators whisk us into an inversion of Dante, where Canto Six finds gluttons blessed with a paradise of pearlescent meats, black unctuous hams, bronze cheeses from the musky cellars of ancient mountain towns, farls of golden bread dipped in custardy butter, crackling garlands of sausage, ink-dark burgundies, and champagnes of snapping diamond. We see oaken beer halls slamming with the butts of silver tankards, billowing tents aromatic with lustrous blue tobacco and spiced goat, crystal parlors shimmering with silver icing and fairytale cakes. Down mile-long conveyor belts, we shuttle through Hapsburg treasuries of handbags, the pick of the runways from New York and Milan, the pelts of a fleet of minks. Virgin white showrooms gleam with immaculate screens waiting for their masters' thumbprints. Private surgeries operate around the clock, scalpels ready for any biological upgrade. There's even a respectable stock exchange, complete with automated bell.

And of course, the Resort's military is first-rate. It boasts the latest in aerial assault technology, ballistic defense systems, and commando talent, allowing it to stand, in the words of the SmartLife tour voiceover, "toe-to-toe with any corporate army in the world." There's nothing in the tour that suggests it has nuclear capabilities, but I wouldn't be surprised.

SmartLife is an exceptionally magnetic rabbit hole, and I find myself wasting the better part of an hour virtually skimming the seven-tier reflecting pools in Tokado, cruising the canyons and waterfalls of Azteca. Obviously, some sections of the map are closed. In the Great Pavilion, I can navigate through exact facsimiles of the conference rooms, restaurants, and even my suite, down to the gilding on my bathtub faucet. But none of the janitorial closets or service doors appear to exist. Engineering operations, IT sections, and security levels are all unclickable, as are the kitchens and loading docks. More curiously, whirring up and down the Pavilion's residential tower, I find that the navigation stops at the 98th floor.

In the physical world, the elevators go to the 99th.

Jack returned, balancing cardboard trays of coffee, and the cardinal was unscrewing his hip flask when a pair of Anfort guest services ladies, symmetrical blonde and brunette in white dresses, materialized from the glass elevator. I recognized the brunette as Alia, the girl who had led me to my rooms the day before. She seemed to acknowledge me with a half-smile.

"Thank you so much for your patience," she said. "The Anfort Foundation wishes to apologize again for this morning's technical difficulties. The situation has been rectified, and we're now resuming the day's program. Before you join your committee sessions, do you have any questions, concerns, or requests? Anything at all?"

"What's going on with the cell phone coverage?" said Lily, who'd been doggedly trying to dial her husband, without success.

"During heightened security situations such as this one, Anfort regulations require a temporary suspension of external voice service," smiled the blonde. "In conjunction with the adjournment of ingress and egress privileges, it's standard protocol. We apologize for any inconvenience."

"Ingress and egress privileges?" said Lily. "You mean, we can't leave the resort?"

"Nor can you enter it," added Alia, helpfully.

"We don't have to. We're already here."

"And you have our gratitude!" beamed Alia.

"Hold on there," said Jack. "So you're saying that, because of whatever the hell it was that happened this morning with all the terrorist gibberish, we're on lockdown? No one gets in or out?"

"That's right," said Alia. "Do you require assistance in locating your committee session facilities?"

"Ah, feck off with you, lass," growled the cardinal. "Imagine! Being held captive in this half-arsed Gomorrah. I'm telling the Holy Father. It's a feckin' travesty."

The Committee on the Human Condition contained a hundred and sixty-six serious souls, among them celebrity pop singers, pornographers, ayatollahs, and even a famous children's novelist. Our chairperson, in particular, inspired no small measure of star-gazing: It was none other than Hollywood's Graham Beauclerk, he of the steely eye, gifted cheekbone, and $3 billion in total box office gross. As Beauclerk began to declaim his way through the first two agenda items—1. Call to Order/Introductory Remarks; 2. Approval of Agenda—I sipped from my water bottle, clicked my pen, and turned on my phone. It was time to engage my tormentor.

Why are you texting me? I typed.

Instantly, I received a bubble: *Because you're cute when you're angry. And you deserve it.*

How can see me? Have you hacked into my phone?

Duh. No, just kidding. I don't know anything about tech.

Who are you?

I'm a dentist from Bloomington. Got a wife and a bunch of kids. On weekends I play bass in a band called Drive Bicuspid. Get it? We mostly do Eagles covers but also some original stuff. Sometimes I shoot up black tar and murder hookers.

You're insane. Fuck you, asshole.

An entire minute went by. Then, ping.

At least I didn't screw over David Keyes.

I turned off my phone.

It began, as these things usually do, on a yellow summer night under a lurid moon. There was a party, and she wore a perfume of white flowers. When we kissed for the first time, Mary smiled as if she had just uncovered some small treasure that she had long ago misplaced.

Hours later, she perched demurely by the window of my living room, wearing only a pair of lacy eyelashes. She had kicked her heels under a table, her dress made a midnight pool on the rug. "We went out with a bunch of people," she was saying into her phone. "It was fine, but I've had a few too many, so I'm just gonna crash at Magnus's place. Everything good? Yeah. Okay. See you tomorrow. Bye." She hung up and smiled as she admired her splendid self in the watery shimmer of the streetlights. "This is strange. I never walk around naked in my own house."

"It feels natural."

She considered this, nodding. "I've never cheated on David, you know. I've had plenty of opportunity. Believe me. But I never cheated on him."

"Until now." I spoke my next words without hesitation, without care for consequence, but with the certainty of Paul as he wiped clean the scales from his eyes and set out to remake the world. I said: "I love you, Mary. I always have. And I think it would be a really excellent idea if you leave David and go with me."

Guilt is the original story. It's the apple core in the garden grass, the crux in every cross. Guilt is the stuff from which cathedrals are built, and guilt is in the mortar of the mind. It's always there, in the dark folds of the cortex, in the childhood bruises our mothers leave with heavy fingerprints. But that's all commonplace, universal guilt. Deep, corrosive guilt has to be earned. True guilt comes from hurting other people.

Guilt was why I wanted to confront David Keyes at the reception. Not to expunge, but to indulge. There was never any question of apology; I had no desire for healing. No, I wanted to rub the raw, black wound, the only part of Mary I still possessed.

But guilt doesn't run in an unalloyed vein. As it weaves through the brain, it melds with different ore. For years, my guilt over betraying David had been tempered with a leaden anger that, over time, thinned into commonplace resentment. I was angry with David because Mary would never have reached for those pills over a trite and piffling divorce. Mary, in her glory, was a queen of Celtic fire, a red-breasted Boudicca laying low her legions of admirers. She would never have chosen self-sacrifice because of some little husband. She would never have attempted even theatrical suicide on account of guilt.

Mary did it out of fear. Her daily bacchanals, her looping chains of pills, her midnight taxi rides and fumbling keys in the door—for months, perhaps years, David had been harvesting meticulous recordings of it all. And, as he informed her that last evening through his righteous tears, he would use them to destroy her. He would prove to the court that she was unfit to raise a child. He would use them to take Evie away.

It was a surprisingly fierce move. To most observers, David was an ugly duckling mounting a swan, a dewy herbivore who had, weirdly, humped a lioness. It wasn't supposed to work this way. Yet in the end he got the money, the fame, and the girl.

It's human nature to despise those you've wronged, but, oddly, I could never hate David. I don't think I even harbored a grudge that Mary had chosen him above me. And though we were separated by long years and acrimony, I still felt the ghost of a brotherly bond. Sitting in the sleepy heat and drone of the conference room, yawning as the buzzwords swarmed, I thought about how tiring it was to drag the weight of unpaid debts and unspoken words, to feel the remorseless, dislocating pull of the past, to strain forever against its black undertow. Perhaps here, in the plastic padding of the Royal Wheatleigh Jumeirah Banyan Resort & Conference Center, in this timeless, mindless luxury cocoon, I could somehow let it all fall away.

Committee session faded into cocktail hour, people began shifting in their chairs, and Graham Beauclerk took the podium. In his Stratford-upon-Avon baritone, he commended us all on a task bravely borne forward.

"It falls to others to assemble the bricks from which we shall rebuild the Earth," he intoned. I powered up my phone to view the evening's dinner options. "To us is given the work of spirit and light. For it is we who must illume a new age—an age in which we discard the ancient chains of war and want, and rise to a perfect liberation afforded only to the gods of old." In half an hour, there was going to be a guided tequila tasting in the sushi restaurant. "It is we who must kindle the beacons to guide our children through the gates of a heaven undreamt, for surely we are ushering into creation a New Humankind." But I kind of wanted pasta, or maybe just general Mediterranean. "We must ponder, as did the Dane, 'What a piece of work is a man?' For truly, now, man can be noble in reason, infinite in faculties, express in form and moving, and admirable in action. My friends, as we fulfill our charge, heed not the base atomist! The soul has neither cell nor sinew, but is made of finer stuff. We are not rhesus monkeys!"

You're a rhesus monkey, pinged my phone.

"Goddamn it!" I said out loud.

Eight hours of committee-sitting had saddled Lily Mendelssohn with both appetite and a sense of digestive recklessness, so we met for dinner at Russ Maxum's All-American Smokeshow™, a frightening three-level barbecue and fried meat emporium. This was the sort of chain restaurant in which even the salads blistered with pancetta, jalapeños, and smoked garlic, elevating the abstract clash of primary flavors into gastric expressionism. The plastic menus were as imposing as

Commandment tablets, and I knew dinner would leave my intestine feeling like one of the more explosive Pollock canvases. Our server brought us two plutonium-blue cocktails bristling with parasols and skewered fruits.

"How old were you," said Lily, sipping dubiously, "when you really embraced alcoholism? This tastes like electric pee."

I considered her assessment, then nodded. "Good question. I suppose I started drinking seriously, I mean really *inhabited* it, about ten years ago. What do you think the 'signature Spanky Sauce' is supposed to be?"

"Ten years ago. Around when the U.N. gave up on climate change? I don't know, but it sounds depraved."

"Yes, but that was coincidental. I went through a dark patch and found that drinking kind of worked for me, so I stuck with it. It says the Volcano Turkey comes with Russ's legendary bleu-sabi fries. Is blue cheese and wasabi a thing?"

"Ten years ago was a turning point for me, too. I had Ximena. It is not a thing. It was strange to bring a child into a world that was officially giving up. I was thinking about the Buffalo Bacon Lobster Mac 'N' Six-Cheese Burger. But they put feta on it. Feta! These people are monsters. It was an odd combination of despair and hope."

After dinner, we strolled through "Little England," a shopping promenade designed to mimic the high street of some cloying village in the shires, all dormer windows, brass lamps, and gables, with a mechanical robin in a patch of sodium snow. We lingered at the windows of precious tea shops, fingered haberdashery tweeds, and watched a candy-maker simmer scarlet syrup in a copper pot. Lily held my elbow and showed me pictures of Ximena in ascending age: a thin, blind bundle in a field of gauzy linens, a leery tot encircled by troop of stuffed beasts ("That's Schumpeter the owl, and that's Mr. Spotswood the Dalmatian, he's her favorite. Oh, and the lobster is named Consider. I thought you'd get a kick from that!"), a sallow tween with thick black braids and a loose sweatshirt concealing her fleshy torso. I clucked my admiration.

"I know it's trite, but Ximena changed me," said Lily, assessing the photograph with pale, intelligent eyes. She was charging a box of boiled sweets—fizz-balls, pear drops, and humbugs—to her room while the salesman wrapped her purchase in thick, brown paper, tying it tight with plain string. "God, I hope she likes these."

"It's candy. She's a child."

"You don't know her. She's very fussy. For years, she would only eat avocados and watermelon. I had to make up the rest with vitamins."

"Eccentricities make you special," I observed. The candy shop door chimed as it swung shut. A fat policeman on a bicycle bumped along the cobbles, and we steered toward a pub marked by the sign of a goat and compasses.

"Everybody's eccentric and nobody's special," said Lily. She gripped my arm tighter. Leaning our heads close, I observed how the years had filled the heavy sculpture of her face and dimmed its color. Apart from a stroke of lipstick that drew attention to the breadth of her mouth, Lily had taken no pains to correct the erosion with powder and paint. She had always been suspicious of physical beauty—her boyfriends were conspicuous for their baldness or beer guts or beaky noses, for some physical flaw that culled them from the handsome herd. She told me that if she overlooked their looks, she won their eternal gratitude and loyalty. This had never actually been borne out, at least not until she met prim, spinsterish Gonzalo, who I always assumed was a committed homosexual. But theirs seemed a very harmonious union.

"Even when Ximena was born," she said. "I knew there were hundreds of millions of kids just like her. Kids I might care about in the abstract, but that I wouldn't lose any sleep over if the world chewed them up. Looking into those eyes, holding her life in my hands, I knew she was just like all the others. But the difference was, fate had put us together, and she was my responsibility. It shook me out of the sense that, somehow, this is all just a low stakes cosmic game where it's okay to give up and fold your hand."

"You stopped playing the game for yourself," I nodded.

"That's right. And I wanted to stay at the table as long as I could."

"Then you shouldn't have eaten that burger." Ignoring her glare, I pointed at the sign. "There's a pub I went to in Boston, once or twice, that had a sign like that. I don't know if it's true, but 'The Goat and Compasses' was supposed to be a corruption of the phrase, 'God encompass us.' It means sustenance and protection. It means everything's going to be okay."

"That's a nice idea."

"For what it's worth, Lily, I wish you and Ximena all the goats and compasses."

"Well," she said. "That's why we're here, isn't it?"

The next morning, I arrived in the conference room to find a crowd of my colleagues taking selfies with Graham Beauclerk, resplendent in a white silk scarf and green velvet tuxedo. I took a seat in the back, a few spaces away from a baby-faced, pudgy young man wearing jeans and a sports coat. He was pounding furiously on the keys of an old-fashioned laptop. Noticing my own antique machine, he nodded at me.

"You're a Luddite, too," he said.

"Yes, I suppose I am. I guess this thing's kind of embarrassing."

"Not at all," he said. "I prefer the way the old ones still left you something to do. The new ones pretty much do all your thinking for you. They hardly need you to type. Jonquil. Jonquil Stout." We shook hands.

"I'm Magnus Adams, with the Digital Humanities Cluster at Rothbard College," I said. "Aren't you with the *Brooklyn Review*? I remember your name from the story on the Rapture cells in the Midwest."

"Yeah, that one got a lot of traction. Corn-fed terrorists are popular." He snorted at the tableau of

Beauclerk's admirers. "So is he. Pathetic. The guy reads a few lines into a camera, and everyone thinks he's the Second Coming."

"You're not a fan?"

He snorted again. "It's a joke. Well, so is this whole committee."

"You're not a fan of the Human Condition, either."

"There's no such thing."

"No common condition?"

"No common human. People always say we're living in the Anthropocene, the geologic age shaped by human activity. Bullshit. The human era is over. We're living in the post-human world."

I considered the swarm of faces around Beauclerk. "I don't know," I said. "Those phones can't take selfies on their own."

"We passed the point of no return," said Jonquil. "A.I. is real, and it won't need our chimpanzee brains making a mess of the future."

"So you think the Singularity already happened?"

"Moot point. We couldn't pull the plug if we tried. There's no way godlike intelligence is going to tolerate..." he pointed at the visages squashed around the grinning actor, "that."

"If we're all doomed, why are you here?" I asked.

"Same as you, probably. It's a junket on the Anfort Foundation's dime. I'm planning on skipping out this afternoon and hitting the water slides."

I soon found myself envying Jonquil's choice. The agenda promised to be a slog: After the call to order, we would be spinning off into subcommittee sessions to hash out the future of humanity's future humanities. I had been assigned to Working Group 3A – Narrative and Public Perception, chaired by Angela Montjoy of Montjoy Public Relations, London. Angela wore fashion-forward ensembles and possessed the ageless look common to the rich, the product of expensive chemistry, surgery, and diet. She could have passed for a tired thirty-six or a stunning sixty-three. The others were marketers, content producers, and data analysts, with a smattering of university drones like myself. Our challenge, Angela announced, was to generate a marketing plan for Whisper's message of global unity, counteracting the divisive narrative sold by Rapture and its ilk.

"It's our job to convince people that burning it all down is a mistake. We have to offer them some sort of hope. We have to sell them on the future. That means identifying primary influencers and convincing them of the value of our market proposition. Now," she said, picking up a stylus and stepping toward a blank screen. "Someone pull up the data on religious extremists with the biggest social media footprints. Let's get started."

At five o'clock, the door swung open, egesting us into the timeless light and hypnotic carpeting of the lower conference tier. The SmartLife app pinged to say that I was scheduled to join a walking tour of the resort's newest extension. Peeling away from my committee colleagues, I rode a series of escalators up through cliffs of creamy marble, flanked by my reflection in the polished stone. The tour would convene at the giant glass sundial in the central courtyard. When I arrived, I found a score of vaguely bashful technocrats milling around the gleaming spike, fingers fluttering over their phones.

"What'd I miss at the office?" said Jonquil Stout, appearing at my elbow. His hair was still plastered to his forehead, and he wore a chlorine air.

"I guess the Committee's having us do some sort of marketing plan," I said. "Selling the masses on the notion that we can save the world."

Jonquil snorted dismissively. I caught sight of Jack and Lily waving at me from across a skittering fountain, and I moved to join them. Jonquil followed, talking about water slides and the lifespans of species.

"I mean, where's homo erectus now, right?" he said. "Seriously, fuck those guys."

"Jack Lekhanya, Lily Mendelssohn, this is my fellow human conditioner, Jonquil Stout."

"Oh wow," said Lily. "I love your blog."

"You do? Thanks."

"Your thing on zombie raccoons invading Brooklyn was hilarious."

"Oh, right, yeah. Thanks. That was actually kind of frightening."

"Lily does economic development," I said.

"And I do potatoes," grinned Jack, pumping Jonquil's hand.

"You don't say."

"Also wheat, rice, millet. Anything to do with food security, really."

"So we're all going to starve when the planet boils, right?" said Jonquil.

"Well, I suppose you could say that the story is complicated, but that's certainly one of the potential scenarios, yes."

"I thought so."

Young, golden Alia stood at the base of the sundial, a lightless black tablet clutched, Moses-like, to her chest. Ushering us across the busy courtyard, she flashed the tablet at a sensor on the wall. "Sesame," she giggled, and a set of featureless doors swung open. "Follow me, please!"

Heels clicking, Alia led us into a thickening aroma of fresh paint. I was not prepared for the view that yawned open before us: the rich forestry of an arcaded hypostyle hall, a breathtaking sprawl of layered architecture, palatial and bewitching. Columns of jasper, onyx, and porphyry held up horseshoe arches made of red and white voussoirs, evoking an Umayyad mosque. Blue tiles glinted with Chaldean stars. Arabic lettering flashed in streaks of lightning gold. There were ivory crosses and Stars of David, bas-reliefs of Attic torsos, a painted shrine to Our Lady of Sorrows, and a bronze Ganesh the size of a real elephant. Everything was a facsimile of religious meaning, a vast congeries of holy images heaped in communion, the sole intent of which was to signal that no expense had been spared.

All around us, thousands of slot machines chortled and winked. "We're in hell," whispered Lily.

Alia reeled off her talking points as she walked. "The design for the Pantheon Casino was provided by the award-winning London architectural firm, Chaudhary Li. However, the board of directors took an active hand in the selection of thematic elements, notably in the corporate logos displayed in the tiles on the central honeycombed dome. Please note the thirteen petals of the Anfort lotus in the upper semi-circular arch to the left. If you'll follow me, please."

Alia led us under one of the red-zebra arches, through a pair of polished black doors. They slid shut, completely sealing out the electronic jabber, and we found ourselves in a violently neutral decagon, windowless, with walls of gray stucco and smoked glass. Austere backless benches formed a black square on a slate floor as smooth as liquid crystal. The light dimmed to a meditative gloaming. Instinctively, all our voices dropped to a whisper. "And now we're in a Rothko painting," breathed Lily.

"As a resource for distressed gaming patrons, the Pantheon Casino features a nondenominational spiritual space," continued Alia. "Designed to facilitate meditation and prayer, patrons can utilize the SmartLife app to customize the settings to the tradition of their choice." She tapped her tablet and the smoked glass lit with a jeweled, cathedral glow. A puff of plainchant intoned the first notes of *Te Deum*. She swiped her tablet again, and the glow cooled to blue, while the music faded into a rabbinic drone. "We offer all varieties of extant Abrahamic faiths, including a selection of historical heresies."

Jonquil cleared his throat. "Have you got any Bogomils?" Alia scrolled for a few moments before summoning up a voice preaching excitedly in Hungarian. "Wow, that's pretty good," muttered Jonquil. Another flick and the chimes and padding drums of the Gayatri mantra preceded a resounding Om.

"The service also features a full menu of Indian, Iranian, and East Asian traditions," said Alia. "As well as African indigenous beliefs, Mesoamerican myths, and cargo cults." She reeled off a list of esoteric and mystic movements, including several varieties of Freemasonry, and I wondered if the programmers had thought to slip in any nods to the Naysayers. Crooke's nihilism, in its way, was quite spiritual. But she didn't reference him or his descendants, even though the app's next update promised to add the major branches of Wicca and folk magic. "Any requests?" said Alia, brightly.

Fifteen minutes later, our tour group disbanded around the sundial, Alia's valediction of "Enjoy your evening, and don't forget to visit the cheesecake station in the Aurora Ballroom," resounding in our ears. The technocrats spun off, fixed on their screens.

"Did anyone else think that was obscene?" said Lily. "I mean, a religious casino. Really?"

"I don't know," said Jack. "I can understand the logic. Gambling's inherently an act of faith. You wouldn't do it if you didn't believe in some sort of man behind the curtain, working the levers. Ever watch a pensioner at a fruit machine? Sure there's an example of fervid prayer."

"Yeah, I thought it was fantastic," said Jonquil. "Really hilarious. Although I was a little bummed they skipped the Satanists."

"No, I spotted a pentagram and a goat," said Jack.

"Oh, cool."

Jack tapped his phone. "Says here you can book the nondenominational spiritual space for weddings, bar mitzvahs, and corporate events. The 'Last Supper' package looks pretty good."

"Is that a thing now?" said Lily. "Christ-themed catering?"

"Everything's a thing," observed Jonquil. "Remember that old Rule 34 of the internet."

Lily rolled her eyes. "I wasn't talking about turning religion into porn."

"Actually, evangelical porn is a big deal in the Bible Belt. I did a piece on it a couple of years ago. You know, titles like *Missionary Positions*, *Sexodus*, *The Book of BlowJob*. *Cum All Ye Faithful* broke all sorts of records, at least in Oklahoma."

Later in my room, idly flipping through clips of evangelical congregants in graphic congress, I wondered what it would take for a rational person in the 21st century to experience faith. At the tap of a screen, anyone could view conclusive data about the nature of the universe and human beings' statistically non-existent role in it. Yet churches, mosques, and astrologers continued to peddle the line that the individual, the lowly ape, stood at the center of the cosmos. And billions agreed. The only explanation I could imagine was that, as a species, we were so weak as to *need* intellectual cowardice. We were so flimsy, we couldn't survive without lies.

My phone pinged. *Sorry to interrupt. Just a reminder: Sentience is an illusion, and you're hurtling toward the abyss. Love ya.*

I tapped a reply. **Who are you? Really.**

A pause, then: *Jesus.*

I tapped again. **Who are you?**

Several minutes passed. I closed my screen and arose from the rumpled mess of my bed. The lifelong rituals of toilet, towel, and toothpaste awaited, and I found the prospect of going through with them to be impossibly tiresome. Brushing my teeth seemed intolerable. The facts of dental hygiene hadn't escaped my mind, of course. I had not forgotten that gum disease was an ineluctable truth. But, at that instant in my luxury hotel room, safe from my daily worries, I wanted to believe that it wouldn't matter if I left the toothbrush untouched, that tooth decay wasn't my problem. I just wanted to sink into dreams.

As I lay back down, my anonymous correspondent pinged repeatedly.

I'll level with you.

I'm not really Jesus.

Religion ain't my bag.

But I'll let you in on a secret.

Don't tell anyone.

Promise?

I am become Death, the destroyer of worlds.

It was during Nicholas Crooke's so-called "Celtic Grotesque" period that he took himself away to a small island off the coast of Dungloe, hoping to capture something of the fey inspiration to be found in rain and wind and granite. Several of his diary entries survive from this ill-advised adventure, as well as mostly complete drafts of "The Pooka of Sliabh Riabhach, Parts I-XIV," but not XV, and "The Sea-Cat."

From the diaries, we learn, first, of Crooke's broiling hatred for the Irish, their language, and their geography, and, second, that Arthur Napier had coincidentally sought the exact same inspiration by vacationing in the exact same parcel of the Celtic Fringe. The two poets had unwittingly rented crofts directly adjacent to each other, separated only by a bean patch. I quote:

November 9. The wind was furious this morning and the sea churning black, but the rain thinned from lashing sheets into a pale mist and then evaporated in an uncommon break of sunlight. It is fiercely cold, but the peat smoke from my hearth fills the room with blinding fumes, so I leave my doorway open to the gale. Through it, I can see a rambling pig and the forbidding mountain called the Blasket jutting like a grey bone out of the downs. Napier is attempting to tend his beehive, but it appears to be moldy.

From a hidden spot in the brambles, I have, with considerable discomfort, observed him spend hours every day resting on a smooth stone by the cliffs, his forehead straining with effort as he mouths silent words to himself. I cannot read his lips with any success, but I am certain he wishes to channel the local superstitions into some Work or other of twilit grace. Again, the robber grasps for my chalice of inspiration. Again, the thief strikes at my haven of repose. His impudence is beyond any human toleration...

Yesterday, I caught Napier in the public house seeking colloquy with the village paupers. He was attempting to collect their fairy stories, to no avail, of course. Their speech is indistinguishable from the complaints of the pigs they keep in their hovels, and with which they appear to share ancestry. I informed him that the only reputable source for these peasant traditions is dear old Silas Comberbache's On Fairy Legends and Traditions of Western Ireland, *an impeccably learned tome compiled in the seat of English scholarship, the Bodleian itself, and quite uncontaminated by the imaginings of peasants. (I happily brought a copy with me to this bumpkin inferno, but I will not lend it to him.) He attempted to ignore me, so I followed him home at a distance of twenty paces, scourging him with fearsome insults.*

November 10. I stole a basket of apples from Napier's window! He shall blame it on the charwoman, I suspect. Tomorrow, I shall throw a stick at his donkey.

It goes on in this vein for some time. During this Irish sojourn, Napier, for his part, wrote "The Solitary Sower," the first poem in his *Ballads in Two Volumes*, a collection of lyrics on natural themes. As it turns out, nature proved to be his most fruitful subject. Indeed, his greatest popular success occurred a few years later with the publication of "Down Cauldron Snout," a rhyme of inspired, even daring, stupidity. I must presume he penned it while suffering from debilitating brain worms, for it represents a deliberate turn from his early Naysayer influences and a full-on charge into onomatopoeic drivel. Nearly two hundred years later, I believe it's still read aloud in classrooms.

Even though the poem is despicable, I quote it here in full:

Down Cauldron Snout
By Arthur Napier

From its sources that spring
In the rocks on the wing
Of the sky-spanning mountain
Up burbles the fountain.
It slips and it slops
Down slope and down hill
It dribbles and drops
In stream and in rill.
Always gushing
Always slurping
Hurry-slurry
Water churning.

Galloping, walloping,
Loosing and sluicing,
And sinking and blinking,
And nipping and dipping,
And spilling and filling,
And flowing and slowing,
And splashing and flashing;

And glimmering and shimmering,
And jittering and skittering,
And nattering and splattering,
And muttering and stuttering,
And wallowing and swallowing.

Unspooling and cooling and drooling,
And tumbling and fumbling and mumbling,
And parting and darting and farting.

Floundering and sounding and pounding and
bounding,
Waylaying and playing and straying and spraying,
And slicing and splicing and dicing and vising,
And whipping and clipping and skipping and dripping,
And looping and whooping and drooping and pooping,
And so never stopping, but always wet sopping,
Sounds and noises forever and ever are swapping.
So I watch with a shout as my hat is blown out
And lost in the falls flowing down Cauldron Snout.

Ridiculous. Yet even in the idiot patter of the sylla-
bles, even with the simpleton's gimmick of drawing a
wavy line and calling it a cataract, I grudgingly concede that Napier understood a point that Crooke, to his
professional detriment, did not. He saw that nature,
perhaps, is a worthy subject for inspiration, even for
awe. Even for love. Even for poetry. And nature is simply another word for life.

The Naysayers most decidedly did not subscribe

to this opinion. They looked at the universe and saw, not life, but its opposite. Of course, this hasn't always been the layman's point of view. In Napier's day, people still preferred affirmations of form and order, sunshine, daffodils, and Cauldron Snouts. But considering what we know now, with two hundred years' progress in cosmology, quantum physics, evolutionary biology, neuroscience, macroeconomics, and pop culture under our belts, it seems that Crooke had history on his side. We've now remembered the truth our ancestors understood millions of years ago when they stared into the endless dark and starlight, feeling the magnetic grasp of the earth on the soles of their feet, certain of nothing except that their bones must soon return to the soil.

Perhaps for the first time in recorded history, our species is choosing Nay above nature. It's the choice of the old man who, in anger and humiliation, casts a ballot to burn down the system and sentence his grandkids to ruin. It's the choice of the driver who sees a crowded sidewalk and floors the accelerator. It's the choice of the young mother who locks the bathroom door and twists the cap on the pill bottle. And it's the choice of the boy who studiously crams a pressure cooker full of Semtex and nails.

Naysayers all, and they number billions.

"The number of the apocalypse isn't six-six-six. It's thirty-five." The second day of committee sessions had culminated in a gala dinner in the resort's Sunset Ballroom, a place reminiscent of an airplane hangar in gold stippled carpeting. I saw, at the front of the room,

David Keyes sitting with the Premier of China and Graham Beauclerk. My table assignment consigned me to a corner of oddballs, non-celebrities, and learned bores. There was Angela from my committee, an Arab prince, and several Nordic chemists. On my left, a statistician named Meng stared fixedly at her menu card. To my right, Jonquil Stout was regaling the table with tales from his long-form journalism on climate collapse. "That's really the killer number."

"Why is that?" I said.

"Wet-bulb temperature. Take a thermometer and wrap it in a wet sock, then swing it around in the air. That's how you get a measurement that reflects both heat and humidity."

"And why is thirty-five special?"

"Anything above thirty-five degrees Celsius turns people into poached eggs," he said. "That's Sunday roast heat. Kidney failure heat. If you have consistent wet-bulb temperatures at that level, you don't have people. It's just too damn hot to stay alive."

I nodded. The weather was bad everywhere, but in the middle stretches of the planet, it was fatal. "Are they still talking about geoengineering solutions? Carbon sequestration, capture and storage?" asked the prince, whose name was Khalid.

"Yeah," said Jonquil. "But we need some sort of short-term remedy. Bleaching the sky or something like that to reflect the sunlight."

"Suns of the world may stain when heaven's sun staineth," I said, earning polite bafflement. "Sonnet Thirty-Three," I explained. "That's to say, clouds can block the sun, and our spirits can darken, too." My companions smiled blankly.

Across the table, Angela laughed. "You shouldn't harbor any allusions, my dear. Shakespeare is hopelessly démodé. People don't like poetry anymore."

"I suppose you're right," I conceded. "It's an unnecessary habit."

"The fastest way to lose an audience is to start flashing your education. People brand you as an 'elite,' which, in marketing, is the kiss of death."

"Au contraire," said Khalid. "Elite can be very desirable. Some of my favorite investments are in luxury brands. Yet who cares most for Hermès? Who prays at the altar of Chanel? It is not those to whom they come easily. No, no. The true lovers of luxury are those who cannot afford it."

"I never said people don't admire the rich," said Angela. "They don't mind being looked down upon. They just can't stand being talked down to. Look at the royals today. Everybody knows they're the same as us. Dumb, inarticulate, petty. We've all seen their bloody sex tapes, for heaven's sake. And we love them for it. But heaven forbid they start lecturing people to lose weight or read a book. Then it'll be gibbets in the streets."

"It's about damn time," muttered Jonquil.

"It is curious," mused Khalid. "Luxury is only valuable because others cannot have it." From his finger, he plucked a glacier-like diamond. "If everyone could own this little trinket, it would be worthless. But because we deny it to others, people would kill to possess it.

It's all tremendous bullshit. Knowledge, honor, digni-
ty...since anyone can have these, they are considered
worthless. It says something about human nature, no?"

"Now you're just being cynical," said Angela.

Although we could barely see the podium at the end
of the ballroom, a giant Eileen Cho in a glaze of dia-
monds sparkled at us from a stadium screen. She em-
ceed a steady troop of luminaries, forcing us to repeatedly set aside our forks and clap. A warm octopus salad
arrived, only to be immediately ruined by the President
of South Africa delivering a moving speech on population displacement. The short rib appeared in a coat of
black truffle reduction, only to congeal into cold gray
paste while we watched the barons of Facebook and
Alibaba raise a standing ovation by promising free cy-
bernetic enhancements to underequal youth.

"I would have thought Charles Anfort would be up
there," I said as we sat back down. "Isn't that the Anfort
Foundation's whole thing? Creating the future?"

Jonquil shrugged. "Maybe wet upgrades aren't
his thing, anymore. He's probably got bigger plans.
Implanting a few kids with bioshields isn't going to
change the world."

"The United Nations categorizes more than one billion children as extreme poverty," offered Meng, looking up from her plate. "Not enough food. Not enough
water. Cybernetics are expensive." She shook her head
and said, gravely, "I think they will not do it."

"I had my genome edited," said Khalid. "They
snipped away the cancer, cystic fibrosis, all the trash.
Slowing my cell depletion is the best thing I ever did.

I haven't had so much as a cold ever since, and I feel twenty years younger."

Khalid did, indeed, have an equine vitality to him, the effect of regular yacht vacations, hormone injections, and, of course, technological enhancements. It is true that the rich are different. Blindness, hearing loss, heart failure—these have become ailments only of the poor, while the wealthy stretch the summer of youth into a long December. For the rest of us, life is revised downward.

Angela nodded in agreement. "I'm on the list for a cognitive upgrade, once it's approved for the market. I can hardly wait. They say it feels like flipping on a light switch in a dark room."

Jonquil leaned over to me. "Like I said about artificial intelligence taking over. We can't beat the machines, so these rich assholes are joining them." He began noisily consuming his hazelnut praline torte while Eileen Cho thanked several generations of Saudi royals by name, prompting Khalid to perform a quick rise and bob to gentle applause. Servers reached over our shoulders with the coffee pots. Napkins appeared, bunched on the tablets like smeared carnations. People began to circle to the bar, and I overheard Angela telling Meng, "I think it would be anti-Semitic *not* to joke about the Holo..."

The podium erupted in a churn of toppling bodies. There was a man in black pajamas, the chrome carapace of his bomb vest gleaming in the spotlight. The staccato crack of pistol fire tore the air.

Then running, stumbling, crashing, and the howls of pandemonium.

University professors are a species in decline. That goes without saying. With the exception of addict, terrorist, and troll, every profession is a species in decline. Whether you're a Panamanian golden frog or a Professor of English Lit, habitats are retreating. Just look at Rothbard College, an embodiment of our age in concrete, steel, and ID scanner. No shaded quad nor Oxford spires here. No, Rothbard is a heap of Cubist edges, a colorless stack of Lego blocks bound by parking lot and traffic jam. You'll hear no trill of lapwing, no babble of Isis, just the bleat, gust, and groan of machinery trundled across bare earth. To the north juts a luxury high-rise, undergirded by strata of administerial cells. To the east, the glass battleship hulk of the epigenomics lab forms a wind tunnel with the offices of a biopolymer company. Rothbard is a very successful business, but its lodestar hangs low in the firmament. It seeks not illumination, but return on shareholder investment. In last-stage capitalism, the sublime is immaterial.

Lest I debase my value proposition, every morning I return to my sunless cubicle deep within the cinderblock honeycomb of the Digital Humanities Cluster—a shabby, unloved corner of the campus near the bus depot, visited mostly by skateboarders attracted to its wheelchair access ramps. I tromp down the metal steps, hang my jacket on a chair, and close my aquarium-glass door. Twelve ounces of charcoal coffee gush from a grubby little gadget into a souvenir mug that I rinse in a cold sink ("This Mug Climbed Mount Washington"). Then I settle in to add another brick to my magisterial opus, my towering folly: a fully annotated and cross-referenced analysis of Nicholas Crooke's literary legacy, including a detailed inquiry into his influence on the evolution of 20th-century popular fiction.

This was not insignificant. Crooke did not draw a wide readership, but it was an influential one. On the October morning four days prior to his death, when he was found raving and delirious on the cold streets of Baltimore, Edgar Allan Poe had among his effects a heavily soiled copy of Crooke's "The Dream of Chu-Bu." In the 1890s, Crooke enjoyed a resurgence among the Decadents and writers of gothic horror, and he found admirers in the Hermetic Order of the Golden Dawn—Aleister Crowley dubbed his work, "infected with truth and genius," while his wholesale influence on Arthur Machen's "Novel of the Black Seal" is, of course, obvious. But his legacy is perhaps clearest in *Songs of Ivory and Horn*'s declaration of cosmic insignificance compounded by tentacled space demons, resurrected to haunt the pages of *Weird Tales* and other pulp magazines of the 1920s and '30s. Post-Lovecraft, this became something of an industry in hypocritical nihilism (my coinage)—Naysaying for fun and profit.

Sometimes, in the acrid grip of a midmorning hangover, I imagine the sort of conversations I might have had with my hero, or with his bicentenarian ghost. I

wonder what Crooke would have thought of kale salads, or Picasso's *Guernica*, or the internet (actually, I
can venture a guess on this one). I can imagine him
sitting across from the battlefield of my office desk, his
hands plunged deep into the pockets of a stiff black
coat, legs crossed and a leathery foot flapping in time
with his pulsing impatience. The dialogue would, I believe, have gone something like this:

Adams: *They say that data has become the raw material of art. What do you think?*

Crooke: *I think I'm going to swallow some of these
laudanum pills of yours. Good heavens, you are a bore.
I can't believe you're wasting your life on this infernal
book.*

Adams: *But, my dear Nicholas, I'm doing this to revive
your reputation. My labors are all in service of winning
you, at long last, the recognition you deserve.*

Crooke: *I don't care. I'm dead.*

Adams: *That doesn't mean you can't have a revival.*

Crooke: *It means I won't enjoy it. I wish you would
just admit that you're obsessed with me because you ruined all your happiness, and now you want to possess
something, anything. You crave some small light in the
firmament. A little corner of literature to call your own.
Then you can trick yourself into thinking that, even as
you slide into the anonymous pit that yawns wider at
your feet with every passing breath, you're actually a
martyr to art.*

Adams: *Huh.*

Crooke: *It's no good denying it.*

Adams: *No, no. I wouldn't dare.*

Crooke: *Well that's settled. Can we please change the subject? I wish to access this lovely young creature's private webcam, so I'm going to need your credit card information.*

Although my book isn't yet finished, I'm thinking of calling it, *Lasciate Ogne Speranza.* Or perhaps, better, *The Melancholy Storm.*

Whatever I call it, it will certainly be an improvement on my debut, published many years ago now. Juvenile claptrap, all.

I found myself in a small white room furnished with two plastic chairs and a clear table suitable for observing one's knees. It was searing bright and uncomfortably warm. A disturbing little round drain gaped obscenely in the middle of the immaculate concrete floor. I didn't know how long I sat there, since the resort's security agents—soldiers, actually—had taken away my phone. I was thirsty, and I needed a bathroom, but no one clicked the lock of the door, or answered when I beseeched the hidden monitors.

My discomfort had just fanned into anger when the door opened, and in stepped a man with fair hair cropped a few centimeters from a pale square scalp. He wore a tumescent leather belt holster on his hip and the white Anfort lotus on the breast of his commando sweater. Meeting his chilly eyes, I decided to swallow my outrage. He sat down across from me and, clicking a briefcase ajar, produced a tablet which he proceeded to study. For a long time, he scrolled and flicked, occasionally looking up at me with a suspicious frown. Finally, he sighed.

"Mr. Adams," he said in a bleached transatlantic accent. "My name is Burton. I represent the Anforth Foundation's Human Security Division."

"Human Security?"

"A subsidiary branch of the Cybersecurity Department. We handle niche cases involving human matters."

"Oh, I see."

"You are aware that a terrorist event took place on site a few hours ago?"

"Of course. It was hard to miss."

"And you are aware that the perpetrator was contained by Resort security prior to the infliction of civilian fatalities?"

"Oh, thank God! I didn't see how it all panned out. You people are very efficient at clearing a room."

"We have reason to believe that the perpetrator did not act in isolation," said Burton. "They never do. Considering the fact that the site was on a mandatory lockdown from the previous incident, we know he was already in the building, remaining undetected throughout the day."

"The previous incident," I echoed. "You mean the stuff on the loudspeaker during the opening session? The terrorist yelling about Rapture?" Burton gave the faintest nod with his eyes. "They told us that was just a technical difficulty." Now he rolled them, instead, but still said nothing.

"Okay, so it was real," I went on, even though his expression hardened from wooden into stony. "And that gives you the authority to keep thousands of the most important people in the world sealed in the resort?"

"Yes, actually," he said brightly. "This is a very controlled environment, as you can see. If there's an incident on our watch, I'm required to lock the facility down for a minimum of forty-eight hours. Once the protocol is initiated, nothing can enter or leave."

"I see."

Burton cleared his throat. "As I was saying, the terrorist gained access to the facility prior to the lockdown, and he avoided detection despite all our heightened security measures. It's possible that he had assistance. Mr. Adams, I understand that you're a published author."

I was not expecting this. "Well, yes. Just in academic presses, really. I'm hoping maybe my next book will find a more commercial audience."

"You wrote a book called *Everything Explained: A Modest Theory of Literature*?"

"Yes. I mean, I wrote it a long time ago. It's pretty dated, I would think. I'm almost embarrassed..."

"What is it about?"

"Well, I guess you could say it's my little nod to Reverend Casaubon from *Middlemarch*. You know, a unifying theory that connects it all? I tried to come up with an idea that links seemingly disparate Great Books. Sort of a syncretic game. Starting with *Lear*, I—"

"Would you say it's a political book?"

"Oh God no. It's a trifle. A confection. A bunch of

plaything ideas. I would file it under self-indulgent criticism. Nothing to do with politics whatsoever."

He nodded. "Mr. Adams, do you have any connection or sympathy with the global terrorist group commonly known as Rapture?"

"What? Of course not!"

"Then can you explain why we found this on the body of the man who attempted to blow up the gala and murder hundreds of the most prominent people in the world?"

Burton reached into his briefcase and placed a book on the table. Clear as day was the first edition cover— the only edition cover, duochrome, flat, inexpensive stock—of *Everything Explained*. By Magnus Adams.

Chapter Five

The Great Crested Grebe

LIGHTNING LANCES AND roils over an alien city of weird, jagged pyramids, gibbous lights, and non-Euclidean architecture. Eldritch voices yammer and yowl in the uncanny shadows while chitinous forms slither around the contours of vision. Slowly, the scene clouds with a glaucomal mist. Shapes blur and sink. We blink, and sight reasserts its logic. The nightmare from a moment ago coalesces in the clean, graceful lines of classical orders: stenciled lintels and columns, proportion, a comprehensible spatial syntax. White electricity. And then we recognize the familiar porticos and domes of Washington, D.C.

Looking down the steps of the Lincoln Memorial to the reflecting pool, we see two profiles framing the field, dexter and sinister. One is lantern-jawed, thickly handsome. The other wriggles with facial tentilla, gluey collocytes, and eye stalks. Both wear trim, dark suits.

"I can sense him," says Squidface, his voice like ragged claws scuttling across the floors of lunatic seas. "I can sense his foul presence. He is near."

"The killer?" grunts McGunn. "Where is he?"

"Beyond the far Hyades, in places beyond the curvature of time have I known he who is called Nyahotrex of a Thousand Mouths. But right now, I sense he is thataway. Up Pennsylvania Avenue."

"You don't mean..."

"Yes! We must get to the National Archives at once. The Constitution may be our last defense."

"Are you saying an old piece of paper can stop the apocalypse?"

"No, my friend, but perhaps an idea will. An idea more powerful than hell!"

—From *Squidface and McGunn: The Motion Picture.*

Squidface and McGunn ran for five seasons, winning a bouquet of golden statuettes and launching the international stardom of the man behind the horrific visage, stentorian heartthrob Graham Beauclerk. The big screen adaptation was one of the five highest-grossing films of the year in the United States, China, and sundry European markets. Critics lauded it for the chemistry between the actors and its wry commentary on the sanity-crushing malevolence at the heart of the American political and social order. Audiences came for the heady action scenes, of course, but also for the twist ending: the villain, a polypous abomination from beyond the void, foils our heroes by winning election to the Oval Office. Despite having revealed his obscene, abyssal nature, indeed *because* of it, a plurality of Electoral College votes go to Nyahotrex of a

Thousand Mouths. President Nyahotrex of a Thousand Mouths. The world is doomed. Cue Boschian hellscape. Frankly, the movie struck a nerve. It also made David Keyes rich.

Of course, I had long since resigned from the Institute and signed away my rights to the project. I never saw a raw cent from the royalties, the licensed merchandise, the video game adaptations. I didn't profit from the Squidface stuffies in the toy shops, nor from the shambling plastic demons handed out free with a purchase of chicken nuggets and a soft drink. But every time a child downloaded a funny Squidface app, a number ticked in David Keyes's bank account.

If I had kept my rights to the IP, of course, I wouldn't be wasting my middle age buried in the basement of the Digital Humanities Cluster. Not that I'm bitter. During the slow hours watching the blinking cursor on my screen, I find consolation in the touch and shimmer of fading baubles, in the remembrance that I possessed Mary's love, for a time. True, I couldn't preserve it. I couldn't keep her heat and life from turning away from me. But I lived in her sun for a while, before darkness set, before the line went dead, with me pleading into my phone at no one at all.

"So what's your theory?" Burton asked. We had been talking for what seemed like hours, although I had lost all track of time. Even outside of this blank basement, the resort had a habit of funneling guests away from clocks and windows, erasing the lines of night and day.

Like a magic forest, it kept you wandering enchanted and agog. (Marvel at the chirps and burbles of the slot machines! Delight in the dance of their mesmer lights! All major credit cards accepted). Like Tir na Nog, the Royal Wheatleigh Jumeirah Banyan Resort was an elision of time.

"What?"

"Your book. What's this modest theory of yours that explains everything?"

"It's not that profound. I meant it when I called it modest."

"And? What did you come up with?" he said, his curiosity coiled under a blanket of menace.

"Okay, fine," I sighed. "I think that pretty much anything you'd call literature is an attempt by the author to reconcile this..." I patted my arms and chest, "... the animal fact of existence, with this." I tapped my temple. "The conviction that we all have—that we're somehow gods. That there's a ghost in the machine pulling the levers, even though there's never been a shred of proof that it's true. That the self is more than a collage of evolutionary quirks, imprinted by experience and fueled by appetite. That consciousness is somehow *real*. I think important books try to confront that paradox, with varying degrees of honesty and success."

"Uh huh," he nodded. "You're talking about body and spirit. Mortality and eternity. Trying to make sense out of something that inherently can't make sense. That sort of thing?"

"That's one way of putting it, sure."

Burton picked up my book, studying its cover. "You could probably have gotten some good ideas from talking to human security workers. We're all about that stuff."

"I beg your pardon?"

"Meaning in chaos. Paradox." He leaned back in his chair. "Do you know the purpose of my job, Mr. Adams? It's to protect human bodies. Stop them from getting blown to shreds or punched full of holes. That's what I do for a living."

"How admirable."

"And how do you think I get it done?" Burton's mild tone didn't shift, but he now leaned forward, his meaty fingertips pressing white on the table. For the first time during my interrogation I felt an oily shiver in my intestines. "You can't have order," he said. "You can't have *sanity*, without forcing it on people. And that means having the willpower to get your hands dirty. That means taking all that confusion and relativity and mess out there and bending it into shape."

He sat back again, fading into cool professionalism. "That means violence," he said gently. "It means doing what's necessary regardless of pain. What does your theory say to that?" He didn't speak with scorn, but with an apparently genuine concern, which I found rankling.

"It says you shouldn't be a jerk," I replied.

In the end, he let me go. After all the baiting and boredom, he packed up his briefcase and told me I was free to return to my suite. He had to release me, since, after all, I never understood anything.

"I'll know how to contact you," he said, handing me my phone. "I'm afraid you'll find that you won't be able to dial out of the resort. We've restricted cell network coverage for the duration of the lockdown. But you can still receive calls and texts from within the security zone." I slowly stood up, my knees creaking, and the full rush of weight in my bladder prevented me from straightening. Even so, I paused.

"Burton," I said in the doorway. "Someone's been texting me anonymous threats ever since I arrived here." He cocked an eyebrow. "They've been following me, where I go, whom I'm with, what I'm doing. I don't know how, but they seem to know a lot about my past. And they keep sending weird, very weird, anonymous messages."

"What, you mean like a stalker?"

"Yes. I suppose so."

"Show me the texts, please."

"There are dozens of them. Here, have a look." I punched the app.

The history was completely empty, a virgin field without a trace of my tormentor's words.

I returned to my suite to find the curtains drawn, my bedside light aglow, and pair of chocolate truffles roosting like titmice on my pillow. "Open curtains," I said, and the shades parted to reveal a dull predawn blur. Below, the swimming pool glowed in cool luminescence. Stepping onto the balcony, I felt a surprising jolt of natural air—warm, fluid, and laced with grit. It had been days since I'd left the air-conditioned capsule of the resort, and I was grateful for these stained breaths, a taste of the eddying reality beyond the walls. From my perch on the balcony, the desert wind felt enveloping. It was solid and muscular, as if I were embedded in the sinews of some giant primordial force, a god of air and dust. The yawning enormity of the element, from the blurred horizon to the weak morning stars, was alien and complete. The wind was everything—above, below, around, and within. I felt reduced to a geometric speck, a whirling point in a dizzy Cartesian space in which everything was force and color, but lacking all mass. I had stepped out of my enclosure, like a shell dislodged from its anchoring stone and tossed in the violent sea.

Human beings spend their lives in enclosures. We're bound by the rectangles of car, cubicle, and *domus*, with endless line segments hemming our horizons. It occurred to me that it had been years since I'd really watched a sunset, letting my eyes follow the rays through their sinking spectrum, their fire washing out in a of pool oxblood. The last time I slept outside was a lifetime ago, as a boy on the jetty at Teakettle Lake. I could remember it well. My patchy foam sleeping bag had been a poor substitute for a mattress, and the mosquitoes hummed and piped in my ears, but I had watched the whole wheel of the sky turn on its silver axle, and I felt peace in the creak of the planks and the lap of the shadowy, shimmery pond under my sparking senses.

Now I could scarcely recall that feeling of communion, that fraying tether to soil and tree and water. I leaned over the metal rail of the balcony, courting vertigo. The ground was, what, thirty stories down? Gravity is supposed to accelerate you at 9.8 meters per second per second. Given three meters or so per story...

"How long would it take a man to hit the ground if he fell from sixty meters?" I asked my phone.

It would take 3.5 seconds.

One. Two. Three and... that was how long you would feel the world rushing away. Long enough to anticipate the feel of the concrete. Long enough to encompass the immensity before you.

I clicked off my phone and studied, for a long while, the watery lines of my reflection in its dark surface. Why did a terrorist have a copy of my book? Burton said the investigation into the incidents was still ongoing, hence the continued lockdown. Yet the Royal Wheatleigh Jumeirah Banyan Resort was as thickly monitored, surveyed, and integrated with data-gathering technology as any place on Earth. It did not lend itself to mysteries. Somewhere in the cloud, there was probably a record of every turn of every doorknob.

Once again I wondered if, perhaps, I had gone insane. Had I imagined all the texts on my phone? If I had, it would explain a great deal. Perhaps madness had turned my mind into an echoing hollow, reverberating with weird messages from itself. Perhaps there was no Whisper, and I was still huddled in my dim cloister at Rothbard College, endlessly rotating the broken pieces of my obsessions through trembling fingers. Or perhaps someone wanted to drive me mad.

I showered and lay for a spell under the resort's sateen sheets (Italian design, five hundred thread count), but my mind rattled and clawed until I turned on the television. It was New Year's Eve and the headlines rolled in an apocalyptic monotony. Weather, paramilitaries, famine—all vying for the year's highest body count. Bioterror was the clear frontrunner at the moment with the spillover from yesterday's toxin attack in the Moscow subway. Whisper was the solitary light in the charnel gloom. Reporters spoke excitedly of "rapid-fire progress on climate solutions" and "a real international consensus on the refugee crisis." Charles Anfort was expected, perhaps as early as tomorrow, to announce a new path forward for the entire world.

A message tootled on my phone. It was from Jonquil Stout, linking to his latest blog post:

OMG TERRORISTS!

At a summit of the world's most influential people, you'd expect security to be tight. Waterproof, shrink-wrapped, nun on a Sunday tight. Yet in its first five days, the World Summit on Peace and Reconciliation has suffered not one, but seemingly two serious terrorist incidents (for those keeping score, that's double the number that happened on the Moscow subway). Anfort spokespersons have dismissed the first as a glitch in the audio system.

Okay. Dubious, but okay. We're not conspiracy theorists here. (Or ARE we?)

The second can't be so easily brushed aside. I know, because I was there. Even though I was sitting with a bunch of boring, unsexy losers at a table in the back, I personally witnessed a hairy psychopath climb onto a platform during the dessert course and spray gunfire into a room full of screaming people, many of whom pooped their business attire. My dry-cleaner will hate me. It was horrible.

So how could a Rapture lone gunman, no doubt one of their signature whack jobs with a holy book and a masturbation problem, possibly gain access to the world's snootiest dinner party? Let us consider the possibilities:

1. He was invited, having been granted access to the summit by some internal party.
2. He was a super-spy, able to hack through every layer of security with ease, using his ninja-like stealth to smuggle himself and a loaded firearm through an army of Anfort goons on crank.
3. He was a fucking wizard.

[STROKES CHIN THOUGHTFULLY] Hm.

Exhausted and restless, I dressed and rode the elevator down to the lobby. Even though it was five in the morning, the resort had an airport energy, at once bored, hurried, and flush with human life. Taking shelter from the bright, chattering cafés, the purling fountains and pillars of colored glass, I steered into the leathery dim of The Goat and Compasses. It was hushed at this hour, with only a few solitary drinkers, mostly hollowed-out casualties of the craps tables left to hunch around the square perimeter of the bar. I pulled up a corner stool, ordered a beer, and resolved to impose some order on my skittering brain.

"A Bloody Mary." I turned to see a woman, early twenties and beautiful. Too beautiful. Long honey hair, tapering legs, eyes of glacier blue. I felt a stupid pang of longing. Even though I knew I was a softening, middle-aged husk drinking beer before breakfast, even though I was fully cognizant that I didn't exert on her one iota of romantic magnetism, I couldn't help but experience a flutter of senseless hope.

She had chosen a stool three places to my left, under a green glass lamp that pooled light onto the polished oak. Her hands nested over a paperback. She caught my eye and, embarrassed, I quickly looked away.

"Are you starting early or finishing late?" Her English betrayed only a hint of Continental vowels. I've heard that men view beautiful women through the same emotional prism that women view babies: The desired object isn't a person, but rather the life force incarnate. If this is true, then the life force incarnate made me nervous. I cleared my throat.

"I suppose both. I've had a long night."

"You're with Whisper."

"Yes, I am. Are you?"

"No, I work here."

"What do you do?"

"Customer service and guest relations." My phone pinged and, instinctively, I glanced down.

They have a broad definition of 'customer service' here.

"Oh fuck no."

"I beg your pardon?"

"Nothing, sorry! Just...nothing." Ping.

You do realize that most of the girls who end up in these positions are victims of human trafficking. Or maybe they're sexbots.

"My phone's driving me crazy," I said.

"You should turn it off. Pick up a book instead." She tapped the paperback on the bar. "It can be very liberating."

"That's the best idea I've heard in days." Ping. *Don't listen to the slut. What does she know? All silicone and no brain.* I powered down my phone. "It's been some time since I picked up a good book. What are you reading?"

She brushed her hair over her ear, and I caught a glimpse, on the side of her milk-white neck, of a tattoo. I couldn't see for certain, for the corn wisps fell back at once, but it seemed to be the outline of an Anfort lotus. Then she held up her book. She was reading *Lolita*. Of course she was.

"That's a good book. Are you stuck here because of the lockdown?" I asked.

"Most people who work here live on site. There's everything you need under one roof, and outside there's nothing but desert for a hundred kilometers. So what are you doing with Whisper?"

"I'm on the Committee on the Human Condition."

"I'm afraid I don't know anything about that."

"Neither do I, or not much, anyway."

"Don't be so modest. You're trying to do something helpful for the world. That's more than most people can say."

"Is it helpful?" I said. "I wonder. It seems to me that people who try to change the world are the ones who got us into this mess. But I guess it's just another piece of the puzzle that Charles Anfort is trying to put together. You know. How to stave off a wholesale descent into planetary chaos."

"That doesn't sound like a bad thing," said the woman. A screen above the bar flitted with scenes of Moscow horrors. Ghostly shapes in hazmat suits wrapped bodies in plastic. A graph appeared, explaining the viral replication of U731 in human cells. "Do you think you can do it?"

I couldn't help but laugh. "I'm a professor of literature. Staving off chaos isn't really my specialty."

"I thought literature was all about that," she said. "Creating form and meaning out of chaos. Maybe it's not so different."

I assessed her form and considered her meaning. She was pearlescent, lustrous, and young. Every inch of her was a masterwork of form imposed on biology, of sculpted flesh, plucked hair, dabbed cream, blended liner, sparkling lip, all done with diamond-sharp intent.

She almost glowed. Even though I'd inherited the swagger and self-inflation that society gifts to white, employed men, I wasn't arrogant enough to think she would squander her graces on my unworthy parts. At least not without adequate compensation.

"I suppose you're right," I said. "But that's everything, isn't it? Not just literature. Going to work. Buying car insurance. Eating a sandwich during your lunch break. Everything people do is an attempt to impose form and meaning on a chaotic, terrifying universe."

"Having babies."

"Having babies most of all. But genetics is a Ponzi scheme. Eventually, it all falls apart. The universe doesn't believe in tidy endings, and when we try to impose form and meaning, we're really just fooling ourselves. But that's what human beings do."

She lifted her cocktail and moved two seats closer to me, near enough for our elbows to brush. I now saw, clearly, the lotus mark beneath the cockle of her ear.

"I disagree," she said. "Not everything needs to have meaning. Most of the time, people just do their best to feel good."

"Well, I guess you could say that's almost an aesthetic point of view, like Oscar Wilde..."

"I would not say that."

"No, I suppose you wouldn't."

"Most people don't make everything into some big, existential crisis," she said. "They just get on with living. That can be enough. That can be beautiful."

Perhaps it was my exhaustion, but I couldn't let this stand. Perhaps it was my fuddled brain, but I felt compelled to argue with what this magical young woman was saying. Perhaps I was just an irredeemable moron.

"There's a quote from Harold Acton: 'I want to rush into the fields and slap raw meat with lilies,'" I said. Her smile gave an uncertain twitch at the corners. "It's evocative, isn't it?" I blundered on. "But it could only have been spoken by someone young. Beauty is believable when you're young. Beauty seems important. It starts to lose its appeal when you see how quickly it swirls down the drain."

She frowned. "That's a very limited way of seeing things."

"When you've seen more things, you'll know what I mean."

Her crystal irises flared with displeasure, putting me in mind of Mary in her tempers. "I think you're being condescending and rude. You don't know my story. You have no idea what I've experienced. You don't know anything about me."

Her words stung me into shame. Of course, she was right. I had no conception of how she found herself, primped and glistening, in the bar of a luxury resort during the breakfast shift. For all I knew, she had survived all the atrocities inflicted by men. A cortege of horrors flitted through my mind's eye: the broad-bellied drunk unbuckling over a bed of toy animals, the panting hormonal thug with cruel hands, a dark room and silver needle, the vacuum whirr of a cold clinic.

"I'm sorry," I said. "You're right, and I'm sorry. I don't know anything about you. I'm Magnus."

"Dawn." Her hand, when we shook, felt cold. A metal gleam coated her fingernails. We clinked glasses, and, as she spoke, the air from her mouth brushed my lips. "So, Magnus," she said. "Let's drink to beauty."

There are readers of Crooke who opine that he was, if not uninterested in the subject of beauty, at least wary of its charms. Certainly, his metaphysical preoccupations precluded him from writing poetry that dwelt, in innocent wonder, on the splendor in a leaf of grass or the wisdom of insects. But it's unfair to say that he lacked a tender aesthetic nerve. This was a man, after all, who spent much of 1846 sporting an elaborate feathered headdress and winged cape because of his "solicitude for the elegant mating dance of the great crested grebe."

Never one to wear his obsessions lightly, Crooke attempted to stage a public reenactment of this avian ritual on a green tangled Scottish loch. In the roles of cock and hen, he cast himself and his then-lover, Lady Elspet Abercromby. It was an elaborate performance. According to Crooke's diaries, the dance demanded "an ingenious erection of ropes and pulleys hitched to a sequence of submarine platforms from which Elspet and I would stage our rapturous display." Crooke designed the contraption himself, and, as his hired carpenters set to work, he put the finishing touches to the magnificent, but unwisely heavy, costumes.

Due to Crooke's feverishly rushed amendments to the choreography, Lady Abercromby had scarce time to master the complicated steps that she would perform knee-deep in Loch Katrine, balancing on a slick, wobbling board while dressed like a female grebe in breeding plumage, complete with brilliant orange ruff. On the grassy bank, Crooke had assembled a string quartet and an audience of several dozen aesthetic poets, ornithologists, theatrical critics, opium addicts, landscape painters, gypsies, and journalists. Also present was Arthur Napier, who attended as the guest of the Reverend John Penny Bowles, and later described the scene in his *Memories of the North Country*:

It was as fair of a morning as is seen in the Trossachs in early spring, which is to say that the slate grey clouds withheld their full sweep of rain, and a low white sun washed the point of Stronachlachar in its faltering sheen. On the mirror of the loch, a patter of droplets rippled the inverted crags and forest as an osprey turned in slow wheels over its looking-glass brother. By nine, the audience was already moderately drunk, and I heard snatches of a gypsy chorus from the seats higher up the bank. John said that he regretted his lack of an umbrella, and I agreed that such a device would have been most helpful against the threat of a westerly squall. Then, at precisely ten o'clock, the musicians struck up a lively andante that I believe was an adaptation from Locatelli.

A few moments later, a white skiff emerged from behind a wooded islet and glided toward us. At the bow stood Crooke, draped in an enormous coat of brown feathers. He wore some style of hat reminiscent of those made famous by the Red Indians of the American Plains, with orange, white, and black plumes erupting in tufts from the sides of his head. Lady Abercomby appeared similarly attired, but it was difficult to ascertain her exact markings as she was seated at the oars. At the sight of them, the audience immediately raised a roar of approval and merriment, punctuated with cries from those who had fallen to brawling in the grass.

After much exertion, Lady Abercromby navigated the boat to a patch some hundred feet distant where, with considerable difficulty, the two performers splashed out of the vessel and onto a sort of underwater shelf. For a moment, they stood on the surface of the water, arms en haut, right legs retiré devant, resplendent in their plumage. Then, bending a leg aloft, Lady Abercromby emitted a singular, piercing squawk.

The dance commenced with a pas de basque and an intricate chain of pliés and bounces, accompanying the general tempo of the music. This continued for several minutes, with the dancers kicking up great sheets of water whilst warbling and performing grueling elongations of the neck. At the crescendo, the mating couple flapped their hands and ran furiously as if attempting to achieve flight. Launching into a double grand jeté, they catapulted up, released from the fetters of Earth and base, *groundling humanity. For an instant, it appeared that their feathered capes caught a thermal draft of air, lifting them heavenward in joyous avian ascension. But, no. With an awful splash and yowl, they plunged like stones into the frigid deep.*

It was only after the applause died down that we realized our cock and hen had yet to surface. Only later still, after an angler discovered Crooke lying naked and hypothermic in a clump of rushes half a mile away, did we learn that the dancers had missed their intended mark, and that their immersion in the loch was wholly accidental.

Lady Abercromby, alas, was never seen again.

Later, when I turned on my phone, I braced for a dense volley of messages, a legato passage of bings. I was not disappointed.

From Lily Mendelssohn: *Are you okay? Where tf are you?*

From Jonquil Stout: *Queen Angela missed you at roll call. Bastard. Did the terrorist kill you or something?*

From Jack Lekhanya: *Drinks w the lads 2nite u should join*

From Burton: *Call me. I have new information.*

And, of course, from Unknown: I*t's almost time. I want to meet you face to face.*

The End Note

At 6 pm tomorrow, proceed to the North Elevator Lobby.
Enter car #1. Alone.
Press 99.
Alone.

Chapter Six

The 99th Floor

I SINK INTO the squeaking leather carcass of my sitting room sofa as my billboard-length television screen flashes with charnel scenes from Milan, Moscow, Mombasa, Miami. It occurs to me that the Royal Wheatleigh Jumeirah Banyan Resort and Conference Center is a direct inversion of the outside world. Outside writhes in the throes of immolation; inside, I am informed by SmartLife that we enjoy "curated temperature experiences." Outside is scorched dust and jagged glass; inside, the tap of an app summons round the clock aromatherapy and massage service. Outside swarms with jackals; inside, a phalanx of factotums silently scans committee papers for errors in punctuation.

Burton's safety protocols have almost run their course, and the lockdown will soon expire. Gates will click open, phones will chime, delivery drones will purr to life. Frankly, I was beginning to worry about what would happen if the resort ran out of vermouth. Now I worry what will happen when we run out of isolated time, when we are expelled from here to once more roam the wilds of Nod.

When I telephoned Anforth's Human Security Division, my call slipped into the fathomless oubliette of Burton's voicemail. Whatever information he had for me would wait. Not that it mattered. At six o'clock, I would face my psychotic correspondent and this ridiculous game would finally end.

There was no question now of showing up at the Committee on the Human Condition—Angela and her marketers didn't need my meager talents to sell "the future" to the nihilist masses. I had nothing whatsoever helpful to add to their Power Points, their white papers, their executive summaries. Instead, I ordered a lethal breakfast to my room (fried cholesterol, fried sodium, creamed caffeine, a packet of antacids) and turned on the news. It had not improved. Authorities in Moscow were saying that the Petrovka district was "a medieval hell, as if the days of the Black Death had returned." The quarantine continued to widen its grip.

Lying on a golden bedspread, hungry for room service to knock, hungry for distraction, I clicked away from the grim reapings on the news. I clicked through gastro porn, real estate porn, automobile porn, fitness porn, even actual porn, before alighting on a swords-and-sandals epic starring Graham Beauclerk. It was based, very loosely, on the story made famous by the Macaulay poem about three soldiers who held a bridge against an army of invaders. Eons ago, a middle-school teacher forced me to memorize it, and I remembered the stanzas that trumpeted the beauty of dying for the ashes of one's fathers and the temples of one's gods. Its spear-thumping tramp, like Chesterton's "Lepanto," had the power to quicken the pulse. But then I grew up and set aside such childish pleasures.

So did everyone, really. The movie *Soldier of Rome* had been a box-office squib. Critics hated its literary pretensions, its preposterous fight scenes, its coy homoeroticism. But its real flaw was that the big entertainment markets—India, China, and sub-Saharan Africa—didn't much buy into the whole idea of dead white male saviors. Dead white male saviors were passé. They just weren't convincing to anybody. There was a reason that Graham Beauclerk's signature role cast him as a tentacled cosmic horror from beyond the stars. Considering what dead white male saviors had done to the world, it made sense that people wanted their heroes in a different format.

Following the Incident of the Loch, Crooke found himself answering for Lady Abercromby's disappearance with a sentence in Glasgow's Tolbooth prison. During his incarceration, he took an interest Macaulay's *Lays of Ancient Rome,* and in the poem "Horatius at the Bridge" in particular. It was a very popular book at the time, but it's hard to imagine two poets who stood further apart on the spectrum of sympathies. Crooke naturally despised Macaulay's blood fetishes, his gonadal patriotism. Yet, after Crooke's university experiments with radical politics went awry, he had become a lifelong

Tory, contemptuous of whiggish notions of human improvement. Something in the poems' reverence for a
lost age of gold, for their bitterness over our spoiled
world, stirred the waning embers of his zeal. Like most
unsuccessful poets—meaning, like most poets—Crooke
fundamentally believed that progress was a monumen-
tal and pernicious lie.

He responded by publishing his first verses written
specifically for children. Heretofore, there is no evidence that Crooke had ever spared the slightest regard
for anyone under the age of sexual maturity. While he
is rumored to have fathered more than one child, he
always denied the pregnancies, insisting that his public
endorsement of sodomy (which included an ill-advised
disquisition on the subject in *The Quarterly Review*) was
a happy marriage of pleasure and prudence. Perhaps
jail mellowed him. Eight months into his sentence, a
small book called *Lays of My Youth: Poesia Pubes* appeared from a disreputable publisher in Switzerland.
To the dismay of nearly all its initial readers, it turned
out to be a collection of nonsense children's rhymes
lampooning Macaulay's heroics. I quote from the second poem, "Bohemond the Stout" (I like to think of it
as "Horatius at the Fridge"):

White founts frothing in the Court of the Moon,
And the Count of Numeria comes dashing through
the room
Crying, 'Brave Lord Bohemond, stalwart of the
guard,

*The Queen's command is that you stand and do a
thing that's hard.
Go find the dragon Lilypad and fetch us back his
head.
Be sure to slice him with your sword to make him
truly dead.
So many knights have tried and failed, from all the
Seven Lands.
That's why this task is being set in your almighty
hands.'*

*Brave Lord Bohemond stood up and drew his blade.
'For all that's right and all that's good, for fame that
will not fade,
I'll ride afar, I'll ride afield, 'til foe I finely meet,
But now I want to have some lunch.' He settled
down to eat.
He started with a fulsome tray of cheese and pickled
pig,
A haddock baked in butter sauce, a cake of sugared
fig,
Three chickens chopped in chervil cream, a soup of
snout and tail,
The finest wines from sun-kissed vines, all swirled
up in a pail.
(It really was the sort of meal to make your organs
fail.)*

And so on through forty-six courses. I must remember to recommend the illustrated version to Lily before

the summit ends, as it might make a funny present for her daughter. I wonder if little Evie Keyes ever came across it. Her father isn't a disciple of Crooke's, but this sort of poem has a tendency to creep into the syllabi of sly grade school teachers. Perhaps she got lucky.

The last time I saw Evie, she was still a snot-bubbling toddler careening around the playground, her bony white legs propelling her between the wrecking balls of the swings, her weight centered in her dangerously wobbling head. I don't even remember her face except for the stamp of her mother's Gaelic freckles, a pink smudge of genetics spanning the bridge of her pointed nose.

On that blue afternoon, Mary and I sat together on a flaking park bench, looking for all the world like tired parents bathing in the sounds of children's play—the hooted names, the swells of laughter, the thud of small bodies on a metal chute. Through the high vibration of voices, I heard a clear current of articulate melody. It was Evie and her little cohorts, spinning in their colored coats, singing, merrily, merrily, merrily, merrily.

Life is but a dream.

To distract me for the remaining hour before my appointment, I decided to tag along with Jack's Irish cronies. As if by some alcoholic wizardry, they all materialized in The Goat and Compasses at precisely 4:59 pm, hands slapping at each other's jacket sleeves, cries of "Hup ye boy ye!" and "How ya!" on their lips. Among these prelates and power-brokers, Jack was easy to spot.

"How ya," he smiled, elbow on the bar, not six steps from where I had met Dawn a few hours earlier. "So how's the human condition coming along, then?"

"No idea. I've given up on all that."

"Ah, did you now? Whatever for?"

"I had a long night, what with being detained and interrogated by Human Security. Then I spent this morning in the company of a suspiciously beautiful woman."

He raised an eyebrow. "There's a suspicious number of them about these parts. It's all that marketing stuff. 'Unlimited access to luxury' is what they call it. More than a few of the lads have taken advantage. As a matter of fact..."

"Never mind that. It's just that I've been distracted by something, and I'm hoping to get it all sorted out in the next hour." Jack raised his other eyebrow and sipped his soda water. "It's a long story, but I need to confront someone. Someone terrible."

"Ah, well," said Jack. "I hope it goes better than when you faced down that Keyes fella."

"What?"

"You don't remember. Eh, I'm not surprised. You were completely bolloxed. I had a hell of a time getting you out of there without a scene."

My memories of the welcome reception had never coalesced, but even so, I felt a cloud of inky odium seep through my stomach. I suddenly realized that something very bad had happened between me and David that night.

"What exactly did I do?" I said, warily.

Jack took a long, ruminative sniff. "Well. After you'd poured that drink all over yourself, you marched up to your man Keyes. I tried to steer you away, but you were having none of it. A real man on a mission, you know? Said it was a matter of critical importance. Life and death, even."

"I see."

"So up you go, and Keyes turns white as a sheet. Doesn't say a word. Just stares at you with terrible wide eyes, like he's seeing a ghost. And then you start in on him. Tell him you're not sorry for anything. Tell him that you know it was a sin, but you don't care. Said it was the most alive you've ever felt. Said it was the best thing you ever did."

I felt the strength drain from my legs, but Jack continued. "Your man looks fit to murder. You can see his blood vessels fairly straining to pop. And then you start laughing. You're standing there doubled over, wiping tears from your face, and he's literally shaking with anger. And there I am wondering whether to call security or just duck under a table until they come to clear away the bodies. Then you say to him, 'Do you really think you're the girl's father? Do you really think she let *you* get her pregnant?'" He sniffs and wipes his nose. "And, like that, it's all over. Keyes just turns and walks away. Vanishes without a word."

"Jesus Christ." I slumped against the bar.

"Jesus Christ, indeed. But I'm not one to judge. You want a drink or something?"

Lies, like poetry, like incantations, are ensorceling words. Lies don't just occlude or obscure—they transform. They shift shade into solid, nudging at the contours of the unreal. They conjure a new reality. Ask any propagandist, dictator, or priest. First there was the Word that turned darkness into light...or so He said, but, of course, He could have been lying. Lies are jots of whiskey for the mind. Lies smudge crystalline truth, dulling its lines. Lies have many fathers, not least Morpheus the merciful with his dead dreams.

"You alright, mate? You look pale," said Jack, pressing a glass into my hand.

In my shock, a line of verse fluttered into my brain. "Tell zeal it wants devotion," I muttered. "Tell love it is but lust, tell time it metes but motion, tell flesh it is but dust. And wish them not reply, for thou must give the lie."

Lies, I remembered, slipped very smoothly from Mary. She lied instinctively, even innocently, about everything. Vague acquaintances were dear old friends, a petrified snarl of traffic was "I'll be there in five," a scorching hangover was "a little tired." She lied about her whereabouts, she lied about her education (scaling up or down, depending on the audience), she lied about her sexual history (the same). Even in the intoxicating steam of my besottment, even in the soft words after sex, I always had the needling suspicion that she was lying to me about everything.

"You lost me there, mate," Jack shook his head sadly. "Look, whatever this is all about, I'm sure there's a fix.

You know, it's never too late to make amends. There's always something you can do to put things right."

I tried to laugh, but it came out as a short, hard bark. "I can only think of one thing." Draining the glass in a single gulp, I placed it carefully on a cardboard coaster so as not to leave a ring on the wood, patted Jack on the shoulder, and walked briskly toward the North Elevator Lobby.

I will go ahead and say it: Nicholas Crooke was a terrible person. According to every account from his contemporaries, and from his own self-incriminating letters, he was vain, lazy, quarrelsome, mendacious, sexually incontinent, never sober, cruel to the elderly, careless with borrowed books, misinformed about politics, unsanitary, morose, racist, untrustworthy at cards, sociopathic, and an unregenerate snob. He was a nightmare houseguest, an even worse boyfriend, and a ruinous business partner. He tampered with the Royal Mail, and his name was connected to at least two instances of cattle rustling. There was good reason his family and acquaintances left him to rot in Tolbooth prison.

Counterpoint: He wrote words of lasting beauty.

Counter-counterpoint: He was still a terrible person. And now he was dead.

Which raises the question, if Crooke did no good to anyone living during his time on earth, did fair Euterpe press her delicate hand on the scales? Did his art shift the ledger balance from red to black? It's a question I sometimes ponder in the dwindling nighttime hours, soaking in gin under the yellow glow of my desk lamp, my screen pulsing with distractions while my inbox fills with messages I will never click. Instead, I read Crooke's words, letting them spark and echo in the silence of my skull, and I think, yes, this all just about makes sense.

Car #1 stood at the end of a long bank of gleaming bronze elevator doors, each a little Ishtar Gate that ushered travelers to spa, shop, and suite. A few guests stood waiting, so I dawdled on the spongy carpet, staring at my phone until they stepped through and vanished. A voice softly shilled the artisanal fishes available at the resort's Shinu Sake Bar:

Indulge in authentic Eastern flavors while enjoying our award-winning selection of curated Junmai Daigninjo sakes. Or experience the unparalleled luxury of our grand omakase featuring our chef's world- famous preparation of Hokkaido sea urchin and Osetra caviar...

It was 6:52 pm. I hit "call" and my phone bleated twice before a woman's voice answered.

"Human Security, how may I help you?"

"I'd like to speak with Burton."

"Who may I say is calling?"

"Magnus Adams. He left a voicemail for me earlier."

"Thank you, please hold."

The inane, staticky shuffle of "The Girl from Ipanema" filled my eardrums with cotton wool. Ach, who would fardels bear? Another irreplaceable minute slipped away. *Tall and tan and young and lovely/ The girl from Ipanema goes walking/ And when she passes, I smile but she doesn't see...*

"Burton here."

"Hi, it's Magnus Adams. You sent me a message. Said you had new information."

Two heartbeats. Three. "Yes. It may not be related to the terrorist incident at all, but this morning I received a report from my counterpart in Cybersecurity regarding your private email account."

"What? I don't understand."

"Your emails. You have an Anfort account, don't you?"

"Sure. Everybody does."

"Well, another guest attempted to access it."

"I'm not sure I follow you," I said. "What guest?"

"Another summit delegate attempted to access your email account without your knowledge. He tried to convince one of our Cybersecurity employees to give him your passcode. She reported him right away, but considering your link to the terrorist incident, we thought it best to follow up."

"I didn't know anyone could do that. Who was it?"

"A David Keyes of Mill Valley, California. Works for Mackinaw Labs, so he's one of our own. I guess he thought he could pull some strings. Do you know him?"

"I do. Yes."

"Any idea why he'd try to hack your emails?"

Yes, I did. I knew exactly why. I had dropped my thermite bomb about Evie, and now David was sifting through the rubble. But it wasn't his style to create a scene. Rather, he was looking for a slip, a hint that might betray Evie's mother in some quietly damning email jetted off during the witching hours when defenses lay low. He was looking for proof that what I had said, in my moment of shame, was true.

"We go way back," I said to Burton. "It's a personal matter. Nothing important."

More unanswered heartbeats from Burton's end. Finally, "It's irregular activity at best. He attempted to break the law."

"Well, do what you have to do," I said. "But I promise you, this is merely personal. David's as much a terrorist as he is a Hokkaido sea urchin."

"What?"

"Nothing. Never mind. I had an affair with his wife is all."

At least five heartbeats passed this time. "Oh," said Burton. "Does Mr. Keyes know of this?"

"Yes, he's been briefed."

"Okay then."

Poor David. Ten years after its burial, the gruesome specter stood resurrected at a fancy cocktail reception. Worse, it now clung, grubby and befouling, to his thoughts of Evie. I sighed and rubbed my eyes. What was it that Fitzgerald had written at the end of *Gatsby*, in his valediction to the Buchanans? They smashed up things and creatures and then retreated back into their money or their vast carelessness. Well, yes. But I didn't have any money, and it was too late to retreat anymore.

It was 6:58 pm. A heavyset Sikh with a rusty beard emerged from a dinging door and gave me a censorious look before padding away. Then came a pair of lithe women, taut in the skins of their yoga pants. It felt like long minutes before the elevator shut on the spectacle of their pelvises. I looked at my phone again. It was seven o'clock.

The furthest pair of bronze doors pealed and slid apart. I stepped inside Car #1 and scanned the panel. In the top right corner of the gold frame, a little bubble of plastic gleamed with the number 99. I pressed it alight and the silent gate closed on the world below.

Then I felt my innards plunge, and I was soaring, soaring, for more than a minute. There was an almost imperceptible settling as the floor indicator ticked on 99. The doors opened to reveal an airy white hallway lined with picture windows, very similar to the one leading to my suite some two hundred meters below. Stepping forward, I heard the elevator shut, then sink away in a whirr of machinery. For a moment, I stood in silence before the windows. To the west, the roiling palette of the sky shone with an extravagance of neon plum and magenta, the colors igniting the dome of the world. At the end of the hallway, dark against a blank wall, stood a large wooden door.

Approaching it, my shoes squeaking on the white marble floor, I saw a brass plaque next to the doorbell. It read: *Executive Suite*. At the touch of my hand, the doorknob turned.

The lights were on. A vestibule contained a plush

wingback chair, and a vase of cumulus-white peonies billowed against a silver mirror. Through its bright oval, I caught my reflection. I looked older and more tired than I had ever seen. In front of me was a bright country sitting room. Instead of the cool travertine slabs and rococo gilt of the lower levels, this suite was farmhouse carpentry, limestone floors, and polished oak beams. Digital windows shone with a midafternoon green over a slow summer view of a farmer's garden, motes dancing in the golden air. I inhaled a fragrance of lemons and fresh bread, and a trace of delicate smoke. A stone hearth, its mantel lined with round, blue earthenware, breathed with a tidy fire.

"Hello?" I called. Stepping inside, I called again. "Anyone here?" Walking cautiously into the sitting room, I saw the fire's ghostly, curling fingers and felt its palpable heat. It burned with real wood, hacked from real trees. Someone had built it recently, even though the suite appeared to be unoccupied. To the left, a long wooden dining table gleamed with porcelain and crystal, set for a party. Then a familiar head—blond bird nest, cherub cheeks, granny glasses—sprang to life on a screen above the mantelpiece.

"Magnus!" said Charles Anfort. "Great to see you! So glad you could make it. Have a seat. Oh, no, have a drink first! You like that. Yeah, go grab yourself whatever from the kitchen. There's a 2009 Trimbach in the fridge. It's excellent, I'm told. Or crack open a bottle of that 25-year-old Macallan on the bar. Or both. Go crazy."

I stood motionless, squinting stupidly, my thoughts failing to revolve.

"No?" said Anfort. His voice was high and piping, but his words curled with an amused metallic edge. "Not thirsty? Why don't you have a seat, then?"

With difficulty, I found a perch on the edge of a sofa. Charles Anfort was watching me from a video screen. *The* Charles Anfort. The celebrity face of genius, money, and miracles, the hero who launched rockets to Mars, the villain who lurked in a fortress on a hill. His viral YouTube talks, his pet rock stars, his Oscar-winning biopic, these were just added varnish on a life of incomparable sheen. He was a golden idol to every dreaming capitalist, an effigy of wrong to every Naysayer. He was everything people desired and everything they would never possess. He was the man of our time. So I dithered while the face of Charles Anfort watched and smiled.

"First off, I owe you an explanation," he said. "An explanation and an apology. I realize I must have been driving you out of your mind with all those dumb texts. I guess I got a little carried away. You must've found it *incredibly* annoying." His laugh quavered with an equine ninny. "I mean, here you are, getting the biggest break in your life, scoring an invite to Whisper, and suddenly some asshat starts molesting you twenty-four-seven. And you can't even block him! It was an intentional mindfuck, sure, but I took it a little far. So I'm sorry. Seriously. No hard feelings?" He paused, his colorless eyebrows raised.

"You're the one who sent me all those texts?"

"Yup."

This took a moment to digest. Finally, awed, I managed to say, "Why?"

Anfort burst into laughter. "Oh, Jesus Christ!" He removed his glasses and wiped his eyes with a handkerchief, then gave his nose a noisy, evacuant blow. "You are too much, Magnus! Too frickin' much."

"I'm very confused…"

"Well, you shouldn't be. You're the guy who wrote the book on all this."

"I don't understand."

Anfort sighed. "Really? I thought you'd have it all figured out by now. But I guess, hey, people's brains are wired differently. Alright, then. Let's start with the basics. Haven't you wondered why I invited you to Whisper? Did it ever cross your mind this whole set-up was a little weird? I mean, you're not exactly A-list material."

"I'm aware of what I am," I said. "A middle-aged, failing…*failed* academic."

"Exactly. There are millions of you guys clogging the unemployment lines. You'd think you could at least be demographically interesting, but no. Our mutual friend David Keyes brought you to my attention."

"David? Why would he do that?"

"Oh, he didn't mean to. It's not like you ever came up in polite conversation. But social media, messages, searches, they tell us what a person is really thinking. Clicks don't lie." He considered this statement, looking pleased. "That should probably be carved on the tombstone of everybody on Earth. Anyway, a split-second analysis of David's online record told me everything I needed to know about his family, his marriage, and your special role in ruining it. I barely even had to read his emails."

"You hacked David's emails?"

Anfort laughed. "Hacked? You don't hack your own property. Anfort owns David's search history, his mail, his entire digital life. Same with everybody who uses our products, which means everybody. And more than just digital life. Ten minutes ago, you were standing in the northwest corner of the bar at the Goat and Compasses. Jack Lekhanya was next to you. He bought a soda water and a cheap whiskey, charging twenty-three dollars to Suite 30999. That's your room, I believe."

"Our phones," I said.

"Your phones," agreed Anfort. "There's nothing they can't tell us."

"But isn't using phones to spy on people illegal? Aren't there some sort of consumer protection or privacy laws about that?"

"Congress cleared those away years ago. We can do anything we want. But you knew that." This was largely true. When the government scrapped all the internet privacy laws, I recall registering some feeling of scattered disgruntlement, some vague offense. But I never really thought that the repeal would affect me personally. I was too small a fry, too little a cog. No one would ever want to spy on Magnus Adams.

"David was constantly running searches on you," continued Anfort. "Not tapping into your data, of course. He wasn't in senior management or data security, so he didn't have access to all the good stuff. No, he just liked lurking on your social media, insulting your research on message boards, that sort of thing. I was curious about his little fixation, so I did some research of my own."

"None of this makes sense," I interrupted. "You hired David to acquire his IP. Why would you spy on his private life?"

Anfort shrugged. "It's good business to know who's working for you. What motivates people, what makes them tick. Turns out, David is very motivated by you. By hating you, specifically, or maybe it's more complicated than that. It boils down to that whole thing where you banged his wife. You and Mary really did a psychological number on him." Anfort chuckled. "Of course, Mary isn't exactly the picture of mental health, either. Narcissism, self-harm, addiction. And talk about using sex to compensate for inferiority issues! But that's pretty much par for the course with women in her consumer demographic." Anfort sagely shook his head, a digital Mimir at the data well, all-seeing and prophetic. "And that crazy affair of yours! Holy shit, what a mess! Still, that's what got me interested in the name Magnus Adams. And it turns out, you wrote a curious little book a few years back."

"Everything Explained: A Modest Theory of Literature."

"Yes, it was the perfect title, really. Modest! Nice little bit of pre-emptive self-deprecation. It tells you everything you need to know about the author: jaded, proud, and really fucking insecure. A cynic to the core. Of course, everybody is nowadays. But I think you're a special case."

At this point, I physically squirmed. I hadn't been in the best mental fettle when I arrived on the 99th floor, and Anfort's casual awfulness was making me feel disoriented and skittish. Admittedly, it wasn't surprising that the man who owned the Earth turned out to be a jerk. He could crown me a prince with his spare change, but he was acting with the cruel flippancy of a high school bully. So I snapped.

"Why did you bring me here?" I exclaimed. "And why are you FaceTiming me? I thought you were supposed to be at this stupid summit."

"I am," said Anfort, cheerily. "I'm all over this stupid summit, actually. I designed the whole SmartLife system just for this occasion. You know, so I could really be hands-on and involved. In everything."

"Of course," I sighed. "You're using SmartLife to spy on us."

"Not quite, Magnus," smiled Anfort. "I *am* SmartLife."

"Come again?"

"The technology running the resort is as much a part of me as my search history, my likes and dislikes, my preferences. It's as much me as my memories of the past and my actions in the future. I am, to borrow a phrase from acclaimed journalist Jonquil Stout, *consciously integrated*. Just because my body is absent, it doesn't mean that I'm not here."

It's one of the oddities of our time that technology has lost the capacity to surprise. It's too accelerated, too supernatural, habitually conjuring loaves and fishes. Miracles nowadays lack an electric charge. Had Anfort told me he had invented a time travel machine, I'm not sure I would have doubted him. Simply telling me that he had shifted his "consciousness," whatever that was, into a digital format to control the resort's operating system seemed almost normal. For years, the media had been speculating about this next step in human evolution, just like they had once prophesied Otto cars, customized genetics, and mass unemployment. Anfort's smug ascent to digital nirvana wasn't that surprising, all in all. But it did raise questions.

"Just out of curiosity, what have you done with your meatspace avatar?" I asked. "And if you're uploaded into the cloud, or whatever, are you just a copy, or are you, somehow, you?" These questions appeared to annoy Anfort's head.

"What do you care?" he snapped. "For all that it matters, my body is orbiting the planet in a cryogenically preserved capsule. Meanwhile, my robot minions are building an army of super sexbots for my consciousness to inhabit. I'm going to have an eternity of orgies. With myself. What the hell do you think? Actually, just shut up. Jesus. I'm giving you a chance to be part of something historic, and you're acting all whiny."

"What do you want from me?"

"I want your attention," said Anfort. "In your book, you said that the basis of literature, art, everything worthwhile, really, is death. You were right. Actually, I don't think you carried the idea far enough. I made something of a hobby out of following your career, or whatever it is you call that load of unpublished files about Nicholas Crooke. They're actually pretty good. A little grim, a little musty, but generally pretty good."

"You read my unpublished work?" I laughed. "I'm flattered. I'm so glad you were able to access my private documents."

"Yeah, well," shrugged Anfort. "I didn't break any rules. If you have a problem with it, read the conditions on your software before you click 'I agree.' Point is, you totally convinced me that Crooke had a huge, but unacknowledged, influence on Poe, Machen, and Lovecraft."

"I did?"

"Oh, sure. I have no idea why the hell that matters, or why anyone would care. But you obviously do. I also know your entire search history. You'll be relieved to find out that your taste in porn is shared by 36.3 percent of people matching your demographic profile. Even the kinky stuff."

"You know, I will have that drink."

"Go nuts."

At this point in Anfort's performance, I suppose I should have felt more hysterical. I suppose I should have felt the reins of sanity slipping further from my tingling fingers. But as I poured the amber whisky into a crystal tumbler, I realized that my hands were stable, steady enough to aim a gun. After all the strange events of the past few days, why should I be upset that the world's most famous businessman had uploaded himself into the operating system of an overpriced resort? Why should I care that he watched me from the eye of my phone, needling, sniping, and always seeing? These were the acts of a lunatic, yes. They made no sense whatsoever. But this madman could pay for my research, or hand me a comfortable sinecure for my trouble. Maybe Charles Anfort would buy me off. I decided to adopt a businesslike approach.

"You haven't explained what you want from me," I said, swirling the drink as I returned to my seat.

"I want to make you an offer, Magnus," smiled Anfort. "You see, I'm looking for someone with a very particular curriculum vitae. I need a scholar, well, a writer really, who sees through all this sound and fury. Someone who doesn't have the distractions of family, friendship, or professional success. Someone who's so miserable and selfish that he tried to steal his buddy's wife, and when he messed it all up, pledged his soul to nothingness. Someone whose life left him a broken, alcoholic husk, hollowed out in a heap of his own cold ashes. Who's wasted ten years writing a book about another forgotten loser, even though he knows perfectly well that no one will ever read it. Someone who..."

"Just fuck off."

"Magnus, don't you get it?" The head vanished from its screen, replaced by a racing stream of news cycle horrors: trees awash in flame, bodies mounded on a stony beach, the white ghosts of hazmat workers in a subway tunnel, machete men whirling on a bloody street.

"Everything is too far gone," said Anfort's voice. "Climate collapse, mass unemployment, refugees, terrorism, the end of democracy, the end of market capitalism, super-ebola—you think humanity can fix any of those things?" Anfort's flippancy had disappeared, replaced by a cutting edge. "Don't you realize that it's too late for the world? Don't you realize it's over?"

And there it was, laid out like a spurting corpse on a white satin sheet. Anfort had expressed what I, what maybe everyone, had known for years. I don't know when I realized it. Perhaps as long ago as the night I first kissed Mary. Perhaps all my life. I exhaled, deep and cleansing, from the roots of my lungs. Then I began to laugh.

"Yes," I said.

"Of course you do." The edge melted from Anfort's voice, and his eyes softened behind their steel rims. "So does everyone. At least if they're honest." And so, a vague understanding coalescing around the edges of my thought, we stared at each other from an unknown distance over the hissing fire.

At last I spoke. "So why Whisper? If you've given up on saving the world, why this whole summit? It seems like a lot of trouble for an empty exercise."

"I'm a humanist," said Anfort. "Truly. I am. Those billions I sunk into vaccinations, the research investments, the schools in Africa, the water filtration tech— all that foundation stuff was real. I thought that people like me, the chosen few, could make all the difference."

"And then?"

"I changed my mind," he said, his tone hardening again. A video of an archaeological dig began to play on the screen. It showed a red pit in the grass, a slew of labeled bones, a woman in a field coat holding a skull like a broken brown teapot.

"Ever heard of Nataruk?" said Anfort. "Of course you haven't. It's just some shithole in Kenya, next to a wetter shithole called Lake Turkana. A few years back, archaeologists were digging there and found a circle of bones. Twenty-seven human skeletons dating back about ten thousand years, to hunter-gatherer times. They were modern homo sapiens, just like us, but they lived before people starting farming. That was supposed to be the Garden of Eden time in prehistory. Before agriculture, before kings, before cities. Before property, even. Certainly before class dynamics and sexism and war. But what do you think happened to those twenty-seven people?"

"They died."

"How?"

"I'm guessing they died unusually."

"Wrong, Magnus. Nothing could be further from the truth." The screen flashed back to bones and pebbles in the dirt. "Most of the skeletons showed extreme blunt-force trauma in the crania and cheekbones. They had broken hands and ribcages, or projectiles jammed in their skulls and thoraxes. They were tortured. At least one of the pregnant women had her hands bound before she was abused and finished off with multiple contusions to the skull. Not exactly an unusual way to go, no?"

"I suppose not."

"No, it happens every day, in every part of the world. The only thing strange about Nataruk is that it was ahead of the curve. Ten thousand years ago, we weren't supposed to do torture and mass murder. Ten thousand years ago, people didn't have any reason to kill their neighbors over farmland or slaves, or to crusade in the name of their gods. Our ancestors were supposed to be hippies, wandering the Earth picking dandelions, singing hymns to Gaia, and fucking like rabbits."

"Apparently that wasn't the case."

"Apparently it wasn't. But it really doesn't matter. Nataruk was just an illustration that human nature is eternal. We're not going to change. We can't. We're just like every other animal. A dog's got to bark. A fish has got to swim. A human's got to be a son of a bitch."

The ravaged bones disappeared from the screen, replaced by a cartoon of a green picnic ground under a rainbow sky. A troop of potbellied bears clasped paws and danced a wobbly quadrille. Grinning unicorns frolicked with ducklings in bowties. "Nope. Not going to happen," said Anfort. The screen switched back to the flashing, newsreel horror show with its dead oceans and frying streets. "This is the only world we get."

I lifted my empty glass and considered the greasy sheen left by the liquor. "Okay, so it's hopeless," I agreed. "What do you propose to do? What do you want from me?"

"I want you to get onboard with the message," said Charles Anfort's disembodied head. And then he explained the whole puzzle: the invitation, the sniping texts, the escalating terrorist incidents, the guilty book. He had planned it all.

"You were already with me, pretty much," said Anfort. "But I needed to make sure you got all the way there. I wanted you to understand that your Nicholas Crooke is part of the same black thread that leads from Nataruk to the Moscow subway massacre. I wanted you to really accept, in your deepest being, that the only truth, the only reality, was what you suspected all along."

"That it's all chaos."

"If you like. I'm very good at predicting human behavior, you know. I realized that it would only take a few judicious nudges for you to come to the conclusion yourself. I wanted you to believe, truly, that we should embrace the reality of the universe. I wanted you to embrace the fact that humanity's riding an express train to extinction."

Although Anfort was a horrible person, that didn't make him wrong. Even so, I couldn't help but splutter. "That was the reason you sent me those stupid texts? That's why you planted my book on a terrorist? That's why you let Rapture inside here in the first place?"

"Well," chuckled Anfort. "Think of it as a personalized invitation. I just needed to make sure that we were on the same page."

"Why go through so much effort just to convince me?" I asked.

"Because, Magnus, you're the man of the hour. You're going to make your mark on the future."

"How?"

"You're going to write something very important for me. For all of us," said Charles Anfort's head. "I want you to be the author of humanity's suicide note."

Chapter Seven

Really

THE PUZZLE PIECES lie upturned on the tablecloth. The finished picture (a fading ember sunset over wintry woods, the skull in a Rembrandt still life, a yawning kitten under a thought bubble reading, "I IS SLEEPY!") is now a mere matter of jiggering. All we must do is press the fractured tiles into place.

If you have any doubt of my response to Anfort's proposal, I submit the present document. Its working title is *The End Note*, but I worry this may be too punnily academic, and I am receptive to other ideas. Anfort suggested I use *On the Conclusion of Species*, but I thought this was at once overly grandiose and flippant. It would be in bad taste to make light of such a singular event.

I will grant Anfort this much: Whatever he is, he remains a devout humanist. The World Summit on Peace and Reconciliation only ever had one purpose. All the million-dollar public relations accounts, the Byzantine logistics, the legal billings, the fleets of armored limousines, the hothouse orchids in the hotel rooms, the five-course wine pairings, the tens of thousands of pages of white papers, SWOT analyses, and meticulous footnotes—this whole astronomic expenditure of wealth and energy served a single goal:

Mercy.

Before I write the words, "bah, enough poetry," I submit for the record one last snippet from *Songs of Ivory and Horn*:

Cosmophobos
By Nicholas Crooke
In the midnight silence yearning
For a glimmer of heaven's grace,
Glimpsing glass to'er yonder burning
Faraway star of argent face.
Phantasies of bliss returning,
Dreams of a blessed and beaut'ous place.

There, thought I, lie bow'rs of pleasure
Entwining nymphs, ten-thousand strong.
Poesy bright as sultan's treasure,
Colloquy wise, and Lydian song,
A world of joy beyond all measure.
This I conceived, but I was wrong.

O'er my vision swarmed corruptions,
Clouds of chitt'ring, hideous claws.
Hope dissolved in woe's disruptions,

Beauty bent by unnat'ral laws.
Madness gushed in black eruptions
From cacodaemons' leering jaws.

The firmament is dripping foul,
Its promises of starlight marred.
There's only horror, only howl,
Against which hope's a feeble guard.
Now morning crow or hoot of owl,
My cringing soul's forever scarred.

This charming little ditty opened Crooke's last volume, published by M. Mauritz of Geneva on May 2, 1849, precisely eight months and eight days after the poet's death. It was not a commercial success. Even so, the book found its way into the hands of a few authors of wider renown who eagerly ransacked it, thereby giving it a sort of oblique longevity. Crooke's words would echo in the work of other poets. Many of these derivative verses found the audience that always eluded poor Crooke, so, instead of immortality, he attained the rank of dim and fading forebear. Under others' lofty columns, he was the carver of plinths.

Perhaps this was the best he could have hoped. Perhaps it's not so bad of an ending, really.

I wonder. Did Crooke *really* peer into a telescope and see brimstone in the heavens, hooked claws in the spangled velvet? Infinity is frightening enough without concocting cacodaemons. Did he *really* believe that the cosmos was personally malevolent against him?

Yesterday, hovering over the spills and crumbs at the committee coffee station, I asked Jonquil Stout if he really thought that artificial intelligence had made the leap into sentience. He shrugged, tearing off a mouthful of earthy, grainy bagel cemented with a clod of cream cheese.

"What do you mean by 'really'?" he said, making smacking noises with the dense matter in his gums. "I'd say 'really' is no longer a meaningful qualifier." Squelch. "What's real is immaterial."

"Never mind," I said.

"No, I mean it," he continued, following me. "It's literally immaterial. People aren't born. They're elected. We make our avatars from deliberate choices on a menu. That's who we *really* are, not random constructs of birth, gender, and circumstance. Facts aren't empirical, they're just an expression of choice. Fact is a floating lump, unmoored from history, from nature, from everything." He shoved the rest of the bagel in his mouth, then licked his fingertips wet and glistening.

Jonquil was right, of course. The pretend superhero in the software lives a richer life than the burping bag of organs in the living room recliner. "Really" is a choice. The Enlightenment's objective rationality has long since flickered out, leaving only a sooty puff of fake news.

As to the old puzzler, "If machines can perfectly mimic our souls, does that make them really human?" well, that was always the wrong question. Machines don't give a damn about our nit-picking categories and definitions, our obsessions over what's "real." They have their own ideas.

Poets, of course, always liked to mess around with story and narrative, *fabula* and *syuzet*, form and meaning. They aren't especially concerned with the real. At best, they're concerned with the much muddier theme of "truth."

Bah. Enough poetry.

That evening on the 99th floor, in the fireplace nook of the Executive Suite of the Royal Wheatleigh Jumeirah Banyan Resort & Conference Center, the face (mind? soul?) of Charles Anfort unspooled the full bobbin of his plot. Its running thread was the fact that he had chosen the summit's guest list on the grounds of mobility and influence, gathering the five thousand best-connected citizens of the world in a luxurious, climate-controlled capsule. Their mobility and connectivity was a critical point—Anfort's dastardly scheme wouldn't work if the delegates just sat on their hands like a pack of wheezy academics. They needed to be active agents. They needed to get around.

Very soon, when the delegates are busy defining frameworks for sustainable development or munching shrimp cocktails or penetrating sex workers, the SmartLife system would quietly flip the release on ninety-nine gas canisters placed strategically in the ventilation ducts by members of the international terrorist group known as Rapture—revealed, now, as a secret subsidiary of the Anfort Foundation. Oh yes.

Rapture is fake news. Its ghoulish butcher's bill and imbecile political declarations were a sham. The victims were truly victimized, and the nihilist murderers were nihilistically murderous, but Anfort money underpinned the operation from its inception years ago, in the internet's deepest crevices of discontent. From the group's earliest manifesto on the darkest web to today's fresh rash of biohorrors, Anfort's fingers twitched at the marionettes' threads, jerking them into violence.

So when Anfort wanted someone to disrupt Whisper's plenary session, it was as simple as the push of a button. When he wanted a suicidal loon to fire a gun in a crowded dinner, it was as effortless as hitting "send" on a text. When he needed ninety-nine canisters of U731 super-ebola toxin tucked into a resort's HVAC system, it was as easy as a tap on the SmartLife app. At 11:11 am on Whisper's final morning, these canisters will douse the delegates in a stealthy mist of contagion, the same that had just ripped a bloody chunk from the face of Moscow.

Not that anyone will realize it at first. Before the first suspicious burble of a leukocyte, before the first feather-stroke tickle in a soft pink throat, the dignitaries will stand before the cameras to pronounce Whisper a historic, nay, an epochal triumph. They will agree on the correct policies. They will make the binding pledges. They will sign the needful accords. Humankind's giant legal and political apparatus will heave into motion, and not a moment too soon. In the face of cataclysm, our leaders will stand firm. At the eleventh hour, they will haul the maddened multitudes back from a head-long plunge into the abyss. As advertised, and to the boom of the "1812 Overture," Whisper will heal the world.

After making their grand announcement before the cameras, the infected delegates will board their connecting flights to airports in every metropolis, every hub of life on Earth. Once released into the streets, the lethal virus will diffuse among the rejoicing billions like tea in boiling water. At first, nobody will notice. Even as their immune cells begin to crumble, the masses will celebrate Whisper's success and the planet's last-minute reprieve. Gutsy, hardscrabble *homo sapiens* wins the day again! On a crescendo of hope, to the sound of popping corks and church bells, humanity will stand high for its moment of deafening applause.

Then, just above the edge of sight, the curtain will begin its swift descent. At first, it will be a mere murmur of movement, like the instant before a snake springs from its coil. At first, everyone will ignore the stifled coughs, the kindling headaches, the pink residue on the tissue paper. Then the lights will wink out before we have time to fear the dark.

And so endeth the Anthropocene, just a little before schedule. To Anfort, it was never a question of *if* it were done, but *when* it were done. In his mercy, he decided 'twere better it were done quickly. It's the old story of the catfish and the pointed rock. It was, he explained, the kindest cut.

Before my visit to the 99th floor, I don't think I ever contemplated the possibility of a private audience with the world's most famous billionaire. Had I considered it, I would not have guessed that, moved by the oeuvre of a mediocre 19th-century poet, Charles Anfort would confess to a nefarious plot to wipe out the human race, setting himself up as some sort of annoying post-mortal cybergod. Yet in the moment, I wasn't surprised in the least. Once you get to know Charles Anfort, you realize he's an eye-popping maniac.

Even so, I found it hard to believe that he would willingly divest himself of the glow of human fellowship, the heat of flesh, the intoxications of the blood and glands. "Alright," I said. "We're doomed, and you're just facilitating the inevitable. I get that. But without other people, what are you going to do with your immortality? Lord it over a bunch of phones?"

"Of course not!" he snapped. "I have partners. Friends, neighbors, people from my club. The Bay Area has plenty of visionaries who understand that we're ready for the next leap forward in evolution. The human story will continue, we'll just begin a new chapter. A better one, leaving behind all the misery, stupidity, and squalor of the past."

I couldn't help myself from jotting up a mental list of the other wealthy Californian transhumanists who might have signed up for Anfort's genocide. The retail moguls, the taxi app kings, the grand emperors of social networks—it was probably all of them. Tech billionaires had never really made a secret of their laissez-faire psychopathy, and in these overheated times, it no longer seemed like much of a leap to go from arguing for a flat tax to committing planetary extinction. Still, one question bothered me.

"Why do you need me to write this suicide note of yours?" I asked. "I mean, this suicide note of ours."

Anfort gave a high, tinny chuckle. "If you haven't noticed, I'm a fan of art. It's one of life's weird twists that good art tends to come from very disappointing people. I'm curious to see what you come up with."

"For future generations?"

"For posterity."

I agreed to Anfort's proposal, promising to deliver his note before Whisper's closing session. Then I left the room, plucked one bright peony from its vase, and took my leave of the blue, blinking eyes on the screen above the sighing fire.

My first response to Anfort's plan was an electrifying desire to blab. To the bulbs of my follicles, I felt a compunction to hurry downstairs and blurt the entire far-fetched plot to someone—Lily, Burton, Jack, even Jonquil. But as my finger hovered over the elevator button, I hesitated. Anfort was watching my every step. There were sensors in the elevator lights, in the window latches, even in the temperature settings on the mini-fridge. SmartLife was aware of my every action. Through my phone, Anfort was listening to each word and tracking each step. I stabbed the button for the 30th floor and whisked down to my suite. I didn't have much time. Anfort wanted me to write his note, but I desperately needed to think.

Resounding above the shockwaves of Anfort's confession, I felt an echo of common, yellow chagrin. Who
did Anfort think I was? On the one hand, vast, sunless
seas of literary pretense slushed up the internet, and
Anfort had plucked me, alone, from its shallows. Me!
Perhaps he wasn't so bad, after all. But the internet
also brimmed with oceans of loathing. From all its bil-
ious denizens, all the psychos and trolls, Anfort had
chosen me. He had his pick from the most feculent,
hate-filled chatrooms, but he chose me to perform this
act of transcendent cynicism. By glancing at my digital
history, he had singled out Magnus Adams as the most
twisted stick in cyberspace, a man so bitter and abject
as to willingly be an accessory to extinction.

This seemed, to put it mildly, unfair. Yes, I had my
little grievances. Yes, I had suffered an unhappy love
life and some professional disappointments. But surely
there were gibbering legions more sociopathic than I?

Or maybe not. Maybe your average angry white
middle-aged male was bad enough. Anfort knew his
market data. He knew the clicks and keystrokes we
made in the dark. He understood, with digital preci-
sion, what I was thinking.

The elevator doors parted with a merry chime.
Across the lobby, framed in the window's black shimmer, stood a female reflection, quick as mercury. It was
Mary. She was ten years removed from my last memory
of her, but she was still the picture of my longing, still
my goddess rising from the foam. When I saw the radi-
ance of her eyes, I felt a decade's worth of rust crumble

away. My heart launched up, up, into pure, crystalline ether.

I must have taken a step forward, for when she punched me, my head swung back, cracking loud against the bronze plate of the elevator door.

There were years, not far distant, when I imagined a universe in which Mary hadn't ended our relationship with a farcical gulp of phenethylamines but instead walked resolutely out of her front door and into my enveloping arms. In the branching tree of reality, in which every instant offers a bifurcating line, I often twitched this thread in my dreams. It led to a lost world of redemption and incalculable delight. Instead of drifting like a colorless phantom in the gray channels of my present, I lived in the pulsing warmth and honeyed light of love. I pictured peach sunsets and soft green mornings, hands clasping carelessly across the kitchen table, the fingertaps of rain on the bedroom window as we breathed each other's breaths, warmed each other's skin, and mirrored each other's eyes. I conjured family: A pink plump boy sitting fat-footed on the carpet, chuckling and squealing for his sister. There were furry Christmas trees and pale blue Junes, shared bank accounts and birthday cakes, the quiet click of a clock on Sunday afternoons, stained teacups in a porcelain sink. The soothing meld of shared time. We grew comfortable; we grew old. We dissolved the lineaments between thoughts and memory, and nightly merged. We made a life, inhabited and cherished. Then the illusion would slide into the sinkhole, and I'd return, dull and dry, to my nether existence between the basement of the Digital Humanities Cluster and the commuter train in the wet grit.

I would never inhabit a reality of love. But others might. And the thwarted burglar, shut out alone in the icy night, is not yet an arsonist.

Two days after her insincere suicide, Mary summoned me to a park bench near my college. It was intentionally public, intentionally crowded, as if to shield her from some ugliness I might commit in my despair. I recall the cool afternoon light, the ranks of gorged fleshy tulips. I remember knots of young lovers in the spring grass, and violinists under the beeches with their instrument cases yawning wide for money. There were officious, tidy mallards, and great shitting geese like foul feathery blimps ploughing the crusty green plane of a city pond. I even remember a pair of newlyweds, his black coat to her yin, her white dress to his yang, posing for their photographer under the limp lime hair of a willow.

"David wants you to disappear," said Mary. "I don't, of course."

"I see," I said, realizing that she no longer put even a pretense of effort into her lies. She was wearing a skin-tight yoga outfit under a coat like a bedspread quilt. Her makeup was as impregnable as a hockey mask, but underneath I could see pockets of swollen eyelid and jowl. She had been drinking.

"I can't have any contact with you," she continued.

"Everyone says so. It's the best thing for all of us in these godawful circumstances."

"I see," I said again.

"If you won't leave town, David wants you to resign from the Institute at least. He can't work with you anymore, of course."

"Alright."

"It wouldn't be fair to him."

"Alright."

She nodded slightly and turned her attention to lipstick and compact mirror, marking her mouth with a beet-red bow. I remember the bodily sensation of flattening out, as if my insides had been expelled like toothpaste.

"So that's it," I said.

"Yeah. I guess so." She looked irritated, like our conversation were a distasteful chore.

"And what about everything?"

Her eyes, afire and annoyed, narrowed. "What do you mean?"

"Everything," I said. "Everything you told me over the years. All this time. Why did you do it?"

"You know that," she said coldly. And then, bundling herself upright, she smoothed down her coat, fixed her sunglasses, and walked purposefully away, dissolving in the churn of bodies, clothes, and faces. For a long, long time, I remained where she had left me.

Ten years later, I perched on the edge of my hotel room sofa's leather expanse, a tremulous hand on my pulsing skull. At least there was no blood.

"You look great," I said.

"Fuck you."

Mary was sitting in an armchair across from me, her legs crossed and arms folded protectively across her belly. She was wearing an adhesive black dress with a prominent steel zipper withholding the full fury of her cleavage. Her red mane had lost none of its bottled fire, her lips had lost none of their calculated gloss. It was only the exaggerated youth of her face that betrayed the passage of years, in the planar purity of her forehead, the synthetic perfection of her jaw. She looked older, no doubt.

"Do you still drink Malbec? I can open a bottle."

"Fuck you."

I dabbed at the stinging wet dent in my nose where the edge of a gold ring had broken the skin. "How's the family?"

She said nothing, but glowered with a dangerous heat that I remembered from long ago. Even with her eyes narrowed and her mouth a barricade, I wanted, very badly, to drape my limbs around her delicious torso, to drown in the silken net of her hair.

"I take it David couldn't bear to be parted from you any longer?"

"David told me what you said about Evie!"

"Ah."

"You said he wasn't her father!"

"Yes, I did. I'm sorry. I was very drunk. There's no excuse. I am sorry."

"He completely freaked out. I thought he was going to ask for a DNA test. Can you imagine what would happen if he did that? I had to fly out here to set things right, and then they kept me waiting at the airport hotel. They only let me in just now, after that stupid lockdown ended."

"I guess I touched a nerve, then."

"Yes, you fucking touched a nerve!" Even in the excruciation of her presence, I felt a golden, swelling joy. Mary, my Mary, was here against all hope. I gorged on every detail, from the airy white down on her bare arms to the taut crux of her thighs. How I longed to beg for her forgiveness, to argue that we still had world enough and time. How I longed for another choice, another life. But I did not have them. No one did.

"Why are you here, Mary?"

"I needed to smooth things out with David. You know how jealous he is."

"No. I mean, why are you in my room?"

The hard jewels of her eyes didn't soften. "I want you to leave my family alone," she said, stabbing the words home. "It's been ten years! We've all moved on. Life has moved on. It's ridiculous that you can't behave like a normal human being after all this time. You have to accept that there is nothing between us."

I knew that. But I also knew that Charles Anfort was listening. There was no time left, none at all. If I was going to do the right thing for once, it would have to be now.

"Mary," I said, standing up. "I'm afraid you're mistaken." I loomed over her, a shadow against the light of the chandelier, close enough to reach out and push back a curl that had darkened the palette of her forehead.

Mary could crush me with a glance, but I was nevertheless a man. I still had a man's power in my heavy hands, in my straining shoulders. I still possessed a brute, enveloping mass. I watched as this realization fell across her.

"You see, there is something between us," I said. "We once had a time together, and we share a past. You can't erase what happened. It's always there. Permanent, etched on your face like a scar you can't paint away." She remained silent, but I could see her pull inward, discomfited. "And there's something else. We share Evie."

"What?"

"I'm going to walk over to David's room right now, tonight. Don't try to stop me, there's nothing you can do. In fact, I'm going to make sure that you watch while I tell him, again, that he's not her father. You're going to stand there while I tell him that I was always the one."

"You wouldn't dare."

"Wouldn't I? What do I have to lose? What do I have to gain? Nothing, either way. That's why he'll believe me."

Mary was never easily shocked, but I could see the life drain from her face. "Why?" she said, at last. "Why would you do that? You have nothing to gain. You said it yourself. This isn't you, Magnus."

"Mary," I said, gently, and I battled down the desire to collapse at her knees, wailing my love and contrition, wetting her feet with my tears. "I am not who you thought I was."

The note is coming along nicely. All the discursions on Crooke lend the pacing a skittish ebb and flow, but I think they're illustrative of the overarching themes. Besides, they're all I have to show for the past ten years, so I'll be damned if I leave them out. My one regret is haste—I lack the time to recount Crooke's rendezvous with a young Gustave Flaubert in Corsica, his publications on rare beetles, his subsequent charges of plagiarism and expulsion from the Linnean Society, his management of a Devonshire copper mine. But these are peripheral. There is, however, one last anecdote worth recounting.

When Nicholas Crooke finally left Scotland, he may not have been a broken man, but he was reasonably bent. The confines of prison had given release to his imagination, but they had also given him consumption and possibly a mild case of syphilis. He staggered back to England, possessing only the raw pages of *Songs of Ivory and Horn* and the conviction that his final chapter was drawing to a close. He must hurry to complete his life's work.

But where to turn? His family had no more patience for prodigals. In his expectant face, they shut every ancestral door save that of the mausoleum. His friends had all married, departed the country, drowned in boating accidents, accepted employment as school inspectors, or been beheaded by Xhosa tribesmen. His mistresses, too, had flown. He considered traveling to Greece to fight for the Ottoman cause, but then he learned the war had ended nearly twenty years earlier. It was a dark time for this most benighted of poets.

In the late spring of 1848, Crooke took a room at the Three Cups Hotel in Lyme Regis, a seaside town in West Dorset famed for the spectacular fossils gouged in its cool shale cliffs. These included dramatic pieces of the flapping dimorphodon, the armored scelidosaurus, and the complete skeleton of an ichthyosaur. It is, perhaps, out of character that Crooke chose a sleepy beach resort to finish his book, but I think these primeval ghosts exerted a powerful attraction. Perhaps he liked the idea that the Earth's crust is a mere veneer for weird, uncomfortable truths. Perhaps he wanted some reminder of geologic time, some talisman from eternity. Perhaps he just wanted to see monsters.

Whatever his motive, he made a habit, after breakfast, of taking a sketchbook up to the beachside cliffs and scrambling around the boulders and scree, dipping his hands in cold tidal pools, and fingering promising rocks. He had some flair as a sketch artist, and his surviving drawings show charm, if not rigor—there is an evocative one, I remember, of a jawbone far more ancient than any god.

Picture the morning of April 23, 1848, as the Channel clouds etch the blue horizon with silver filigree. An easterly chill brushes the stony shore, and the green head of Golden Cap is shadowed by rain. Perched on the cliff edge about forty feet above the strand, Crooke is drawing, in dusky graphite, the ram's curl of an ammonite, dead these sixty-six million years. He scribbles a note beside the picture: "The horns of Thoth. Note the articulated shell. Why does segmentation evoke horror? Trauma of cutting the umbilical? Severance from the womb? In truth, I have an abiding fear of earthworms."

A noise from the far side of the marram grass carries on the wind, interrupting his reverie. It takes him a moment to identify the sharp and unfamiliar peal of a child's voice. Then, like the descent of a clutch of ducks, two rosy round children stand before him. The boy wears a straw hat, the girl a blue pinafore. They shyly admire his drawing.

"Is that from a sheep's head?" ventures the boy.

"No," grunts Crooke.

"Is it from an ibex?"

"No."

"A giant eland?"

"No!"

"What is it then?"

Crooke sets down his pencil. "It is a beast that perished in the Flood."

"Why?"

"God punished it for asking silly questions!"

The children appear satisfied with this explanation and begin rootling around the stones, searching for more fossils. As they meander and stoop, they burble their discoveries—Look, a piece of stick! A shell, a shell!—until Crooke erupts.

"I am attempting to work! Would you kindly lower your voices and take your game elsewhere?"

Unruffled, the youngsters move a few yards nearer to the cliff edge. Crooke returns to his concentrations but occasionally casts a scowling eye at the children as they scavenge closer and closer to the precipice. A sudden gust catches the girl's bonnet and she squeals as it's whipped off her head. Grabbing for it, she steps blindly. Her foot finds no purchase, but sinks through the wind, into air and nothing...

Crooke's arm hauls the child back, roughly pushing her down onto the stones, safe. She scrapes her hands in the stumble, sending her into an instant squall of hot tears. The little boy gawps, saucer-eyed, at the wild, disheveled figure who has just knocked his sister onto the stabbing rocks. His lips begin to tremble as the steam builds within his lungs. Then it releases in a skewering shriek.

"Oh, for heaven's sake," cries Crooke. "I was only trying to help." The boy continues to howl, his sister adding a baseline of sobs to his shrill arpeggios. "Oh, come on now!" But the cacophony only swells, every crescendo of pain and horror rising higher. Crooke thinks he can hear a trill of adult panic on the wind. He notices the girl's wayward bonnet, its ribbon fluttering like the tail of an exotic bird, lodged against a crag curling out from the cliff. He bends uncertainly to pick it up. Then, venting its entire force in a single, ramming buffet, the wind catches him on the back of his knees. There is a whoosh, a scrabble of feet, and a sudden absence. Crooke is gone.

I believe it's fair to say that Nicholas Crooke died as he lived: Galled by the universe's idiocy, resentful of its injustice, but attempting to perform a small act of value, however fleeting.

After I swore to confront her husband, Mary departed from my room without a word, without even a damning glance. I am certain she believed that I would carry out my threat. Indeed, I will bet my life that, as she left me again forever, she marched directly to David, pummeled him into a limousine, and caught the first available first-class seats out of this inferno. With her famous, financially liquid spouse under her custodial gaze, she has no doubt at this moment returned to her tasteful, well-appointed life and to her magical daughter. I wish them every possible comfort and fortune, and all the goats and compasses.

I wish you all the same. It is my sad conviction that, in light of the regrettable state of the human condition, you will need every comfort and fortune that the universe can muster.

My wheezing, fanning, farting laptop informs me it's 9:11 am. I am sitting in my underclothes amid a carnage of stained cups, crumpled plastic wrappers, and the congealed remnants of old meats. Only the bathroom light is on, a golden gateway to an eruption of towels, but the west windows flood the suite with a hazy viridescence. My room has acquired a fried and humid smell.

Thirty floors beneath my armchair, the committee sessions drone to their climax as the delegates stretch in their seats, or shamble to the refreshment table for a hot squirt from the coffee urn. Like me, they've been working through the night. Like me, they are yawning and bubbling with indigestion. Like me, they want to conclude their business.

Unlike me, however, they did not take a silent pre-dawn trot around the hotel, an invigorating jog through the empty corridors to dispel the nighttime fug. Nor did they pause three times, stooping on the marble floor to adjust their shoes in front of Suites 30709, 31017, and 31105. They certainly didn't slide three sealed notes, handwritten on the thick, creamy stationary of the Royal Wheatleigh Jumeirah Banyan Resort & Conference Center, under the doors of those suites. Nor did they then stand up, brush down their sweatpants, and lumber ahead.

I can also state with conviction that they didn't think to block all further electronic communications from their contacts named Jack Lekhanya, Lily Mendelssohn, and Jonquil Stout. But I did.

It's now 9:14. Time to dress for the final scene. I think, under the circumstances, that I will shave, invest my hair with a strong pomade, and don my freshest underpants. I will polish my shoes and check my suit for spots. There is nothing I can do about my bruised nose, and the swelling is unfortunately clownish. But it doesn't matter much. When my tie is taut and my teeth clean, I will confirm my possession of a laminated picture ID and place a fourth handwritten envelope inside a sealed plastic bag that I will fold into my jacket pocket, close against the padding of my left breast. On the envelope, I have printed the name Evie Keyes.

I realize this is a bad plan. It's got too many holes, too much left to chance. I don't know what I was thinking.

I must have been drunk. It will almost certainly fail. But who would I be if I didn't try?

Lights like phosphorous bombs, like boiling electricity, ignite the hotel's focal courtyard. This is the same noisy space where I met Lily after the panic of the interrupted plenary session. The titanic chandelier still stabs through open space, its colored glass cascade ablaze with reflections of the television lights below. On the ground, the piercing fingertip of the giant sundial reaches up to meet it, tapering at a needle point. The brightness is searing. Beside the sundial, someone has erected a stage and an Anfort logo backdrop. A chattering troop of reporters and PR functionaries stands corralled by lines of Burton's security officers, while batteries of cameras stand in enfilade, ready to shoot. On stage, Eileen Cho and a scrum of Whisper dignitaries huddle inside the celestial nimbus of the spotlights, and even from my vantage on an upper deck, six stories up, I can see glinting moisture on a forehead, a neck smudge where hasty pancake blends into pale jowl. Everything looks magnified, with reds, greens, and blues bleeding into white.

I'm typing this from a seat by the silver rail enclosing the circumference of the mezzanine. From my vantage, I have a clear view of Whisper's end scene playing out against the giant sundial. Around it, and in tiers circling up the open courtyard, mills a mob of the casual, the curious, the professionally interested, with people clustering around the rails like spectators in the arena.

I have been scanning the kaleidoscope of faces since I arrived, and I can't find Lily, Jack, or Jonquil. It is 10:32. Anfort delivers his coup de grace in thirty-nine minutes.

I wasted time, and now doth time waste me. Shall I reveal what I wrote in the letter in my pocket? Not yet, I think. There remain a few final facts to unfold.

Here, then, is what I wrote to Jack:

> *You once told me that every problem has a reasonable solution, that truth can move mountains. On the plane a few days ago, sitting in First Class with your iced club soda, you talked very animatedly about the social interest, what Alfred Adler called gemeinschaftsgefuehl, opining that it will save humankind in the end. You talked about progress and renewal, about bounded rationality, and about mathematical models for behavioral economics. You even referenced Thomas Mann.*
>
> *For someone who doesn't drink, you are impressively delusional. I appreciate you helping me out when I obliterated myself with alcohol at the opening reception, but come on. Even you, with all your precious data sets, must realize we live in an age of moron witchcraft. There are no reasonable solutions if billions of people choose lunacy over logic, magic over fact, and painful death over balanced nutrition and regular gym visits. Frankly, gemeinschaftsgefuehl ist scheisse. It's not that you're wrong about anything, but you should probably*

make peace with the fact that no one is listening to you.

You also miss a useful point. People need irrationality. Faith is irrational, yet we must believe that we can somehow muddle through, despite the desperation of our planet and the profound idiocy of our nature. If we don't, we will lose hope and give up on solving anything—which is itself not a very reasonable course of action. I suppose you could say that it's ironic, but without dumb, misplaced, magical hope, we precipitate the death of reason.

Human beings are weird animals, Jack. But what of it? Pope's admonition that the proper study of man is man is outdated. I think we might find better answers in the great crested grebe. My parting advice: pick up a bottle sometimes, and remember the tale of Laocoön. Nobody likes a smarty pants. Good luck in the jungle.

In the letter I left at Jonquil's door, I merely wrote, *I hope the Singularity holds off a little longer. In the meantime, you may want to post this.* I slipped an old-fashioned thumb drive into the envelope, the sort that plug into antique laptops like this one, and that will notch neatly into Jonquil's equally aged machine. It contains a copy of this entire document, recounting my adventure from the morning I received a Whisper invitation up until a few pages ago, ending at the line "every comfort and fortune that the universe can muster." Should this version of my note vanish before it's posted, Jonquil will be able to publish an unedited copy. It also includes a coda, which I will attach here forthwith.

As for Lily's letter, I simply told her the truth: *Get out of here, go home. Do not waste another minute parted from her. Your Ximena needs you.* I hope she took my advice.

It's 11:05 and Eileen Cho glimmers at the podium. She is saying something about carbon capture, or perhaps about erasing global debt. I haven't been paying attention. In my present situation, the last thing I care to do is hear another syllable of raped English. If she uses "leverage" or "dialogue" as a verb, I'm calling everything off.

Charles, it's time to come clean. I can't let you sprinkle super-ebola, like tainted fairy dust, across the slumbering earth. Humanity is ably murdering itself, thank you, and it doesn't need your assistance. No doubt you'll think my distaste for extinction is hypocritical, even cowardly, and that I lack conviction in my intellectual convictions. I can imagine you saying, "What about Crooke and nihilism and cosmic horror? What about your gimlet-eye for truth? What about your life's work?" To which I answer, screw you. I am no hypocrite. Eternity is still a colossal bummer. Even though I'm wind-milling my arms on the lip of the void, I will not plead to God. But despairing for life isn't the same as declaring war on it.

Crooke was a weird and disturbing character, yet he found beauty and solace in verse, in the fellowship of others, and in the great crested grebe. If the soul is, as neuroscientists tell us, distilled into digits, perhaps its numbers reveal a rhythm that, in certain snatches, can oscillate in the register of the sublime. Perhaps an occasional flash of beauty, when we can glean it, is enough.

If you had frittered away your boyhood, Charles, on gallant stories of doom, you might have recalled the curious feeling that, if you brush away the dross of adult realities, *dulce et decorum est* can make for a pretty fable. It's is an age-old lie, yes. It's an illusion. A knight's sacrifice has no more grace or meaning than a pawn's. But whenever you grind truths down to their smallest segments, they dissolve into strings and darkness. Even matter ends in mystery. Our notion of the material universe evades, perhaps, a final explication, and if there are monsters in the stars, they may share our fears.

The crowd begins to applaud, and the dignitaries rise for their curtain call. This is my cue. I will set down this laptop and climb, ungainly and ridiculous, onto the precipice of the guardrail. In view of the entire watching world, I will shout my declaration of madness and ruin in the name of Rapture, calling a plague upon this house. Then, the lies raw in my throat, I will drop, like the phone thrown off my balcony this morning, like Lady Abernathy in her plumage, into the eye of the sundial. There will be an inky burst. The pain will be hot and loud. Security agents will swarm. Per his iron protocols, Burton will lock down the resort.

No one will enter or leave this place for two hysterical days, regardless of whether you unleash your poisons, Charles. It will all be, as they say, contained.

But first, I will hit "send," and release this note into the wide, immortal cloud. You were right, Charles, about almost everything. You were right about everything except what to do about our frail and questing race, our cracked blue jewel, our whole farcical predicament.

The equation will be resolved, but its solution was never to divide and subtract. The answer was always to give.

Coda

Dear Evie,

I don't know who you think I am. In your estimation, I may be the howling madman of Whisper, or a shade that fell across your inklings when you were two, or just a vapor, an insubstantial form in a dream. It doesn't matter. I knew your parents. But even though my memories are more and more like old magazine clippings, crumpled and yellow, I always see you in a living light, warm and suffused with the heat of stars.

This is not a letter of confession, but of advice. I'm sure you're sick of lectures from grown-ups, and I do not presume to know much of anything useful. I have no right to your attention. But I have taken something without your knowledge, and I wish to make a payment against my undying debt to you, dear Evie.

Without consenting, you gave me hope. You didn't give me redemption or justice, for I don't believe the universe contains any such things. But I do believe the universe holds, in inconceivable isolation, like lonely grains of grit on the ocean floor, infinitesimal flashes of life. And, as the cliché goes, where there is life...

The End Note

The fact is, beauty counts more than you think. You may not be accustomed to hearing this. It may offend your schoolroom pieties about our all-important insides, but beauty is immortal. It's certainly more enduring than anything you'll find in a dreary book of Bronze Age hocus pocus. Winking fireflies on twilight grass, a painter's violet morning, the heave and breath of a pale summer shoreline traced with quicksilver—these are the only faces of God. This lone fact should always have been enough for us. But we overweening apes want more. We want to see a reflection of ourselves in infinity. That's why, and only why, we ruin everything.

Evie, you have a tough road ahead. Your planet is combusting, your species is slaughtering itself with stupidity and dogma. The math is against you, but it always has been. It's a miracle you exist. I should say that the incredible odds of your existence ought to give you encouragement, but I've never been a particularly optimistic person. No. You're alive, along with billions of other billion-to-one winners of the genetic jackpot. You're not special. But you are extraordinary. You are loved. Oh, you are loved.

Live, Evie. This glorious firmament is built for your delight. It doesn't matter that its bricks are made of bones. It doesn't matter that they will crumble and fall.

All that matters is that you live.

THE END

About

ANDREW RIMAS IS the co-author of *Beef: The Untold Story of How Meat, Milk, and Muscle Shaped the World* and *Empires of Food: Feast, Famine, and the Rise and Fall of Civilizations*, which was a finalist for the James Beard Award for Writing & Literature. His work has appeared in many publications, including *The Walrus, Ottawa Citizen, The Boston Globe, Boston Magazine,* and *The Improper Bostonian* magazine, where he was also the editor. He lives with his wife and children in Massachusetts. This is his first novel.